The Express Squad- The Killer Hunt.

By Christine D'Sylva

These are the books I have written and available on Amazon.

1 It's Great to be Alive.

2The Millionaire Meets the Flower Lady.

3 Bollywood Badshah.

4 Be a Modern Heroine.

5 Unexpected Blessings; a Love Story.

6 Nearer my God to Thee.

7 Angel of Death.

8 Somewhere over the Rainbow.

9 Dance to the end of Love.

10 Soulmates and Heartaches- 11 Short Stories.

11 Haunting Obsession.

12 The Stalker.

13 To Snare a Killer.

14 Lonely Hearts

15 Vanished.

16 Burn.

17 Queen of Swords

18 Maze of Betrayal

19 Web of Deception.

20 Bollywood Twilight

Story 1

The Case of the Anxious Beauty Queen.

Ch1

The Director General Verma read his latest e mail with concentration.

He pursed his lips.

He sat thoughtfully in his swivel chair, his hands on his teak desk, and after a few minutes came to a decision.

He was a very decisive man, not given into rash impulses but carefully considered every decision he made. He had not risen to the topmost rank in his office based on impulsiveness but rather on his field record and his analytical mind.

He pressed the buzzer and his secretary's voice filtered through the speaker.

He said, "I want Inspector Sean Fernandez and Inspector Sheena Rai in my office, pronto."

"Yes, sir, they will be contacted at once." The cool, efficient tones of his assistant, Mohini was always reassuring. If she promised something, it was a done deal.

He settled back on his armchair, his fingers playing idly with the paperweight.

A tall man with a shock of raven hair that miraculously never greyed despite him being in his late fifties, he was by no means handsome but he definitely had a presence that was a bit intimidating. Looking at him, with his square chiselled jaw and his rather hard penetrating eyes, one knew he was a man to contend with.

Minutes later, the cool tones of his assistant Mohini, came through, "They are here, sir. Shall I send them in?"

"Yes, of course."

He sat in a ramrod straight position now, his slightly relaxed stance evaporating.

He looked what he was- tough and in control. The mantle of authority sat well on his rather broad shoulders.

The door opened a few seconds later and two people walked in. First Inspector Sheena Rai walked in because Inspector Sean believed in the dictum ladies first, then Inspector Sean Fernandez followed.

He looked at both with his penetrating stare designed to put even the toughest guy in discomfort. But the two had impassive faces as they met his stare equably. They were never easily rattled. Their job had given them a mantle of confidence and a certain cynical demeanour.

He liked both of them but in his line he tried hard never to play favourites. But the confidence he had in them was revealed by the sudden slight softening of his tone as he gestured, "Sit down, please."

There were two hard backed chairs facing his desk and they both sat down.

They sat straight, their eyes on him, their stance respectful.

He flicked the front page of the newspapers in front of them, "Take a look at that."

Inspector Sean Fernandez picked up the newspapers and held it so his partner could read it.

After a few minutes they both looked up at him, "Yes, sir. We heard this story. It's making news every day."

"Yeah, it's a big story and we deal with only the big cases, you know that. Now, it appears that we are invited to step in. The police in Mumbai are working hard on the case but they seem to have no success. It has been a month now and the Central Government wants answers. Fortunately, we have obtained the permission of the Mumbai State government to intervene. As you know we have to work parallel with the concerned police department. Playing a lone hand is never advisable. I do not need to spell it out but you two know the rules."

"Yes, sir." They replied almost in unison.

"Now, I want both of you to get your asses out there to Mumbai. The flight will be tomorrow at nine. You will work with Inspector Rane, a tough clever cop but somehow unable to solve this case."

Director General Verma continued, "The case is a big one involving a beauty queen and the public will not rest till they get answers. So the pressure is on. I want you both to do your best in solving the case. Do not let me down. We have a reputation to protect. Of late, the CBI has been getting loads of flak about our ineptitude because of our disastrous failure in solving the case of that child's murder. It remained a cold case. Inspector Singh did his best but could not solve it satisfactorily. It happened three years ago but nobody forgets failure. So I have assigned both of you on this new case and I want answers. Now move your asses and begin making preparations for tomorrow. There is enough resentment when the concerned police department cannot solve a case so being courteous pays off. You will stay at the guest house. There are separate rooms in the guest house of course. Please work in collaboration with the Mumbai police. You know we can never afford to ruffle any feathers. When we work in co-operation, things go well."

He paused and said with a small sigh, "Why the hell am I telling you this? You both know the ropes but a little reminder now and then never hurts."

He shoved a slip of paper towards them, "This is the new guest house address. Both of you will stay here. I heard it's very comfortable."

He said, "Well, get on with it. Wish you luck."

The two of them got to their feet, "Yes, sir."

Inspector Sean Fernandez pocketed the slip of paper.

They turned to leave but not before Director General Verma drawled, "You two are called the Express Squad because you work fast and well together. Now do not let me or the organisation down. I will expect written reports now and then. You know the protocol."

"Yes, sir." Inspector Sean Fernandez said, looking serious.

Director General Verma watched as they left his office.

He then busied himself with the new e mails that he had to reply to. As far as he was concerned, his work with them at present at least, was over.

Ch 2

The CBI or the Central Board of Investigation is the premier investigating agency of India. It was originally set up to investigate bribery and governmental corruption. The CBI is officially designated as the single point of contact for liaison with the Interpol.

The motto of the CBI is- Industry, Impartiality and Integrity that must always guide their work.

The CBI is equivalent to the American FBI.

In the past casual dress such as jeans and T shirts were tolerated at the workplace but Director Verma was a stickler for formality and he had announced that no informal dress code would be entertained at least at the workplace. But during investigative procedures, this was permitted for often the officers had to blend in with the public.

The officers of the higher level were permitted to carry guns.

The next morning, Inspector Sean Fernandez and Inspector Sheena Rai boarded the Indian Airlines flight that would take them to Mumbai.

They had adjacent seats on the plane.

Both were dressed casually, although both also carried guns. This was permitted for they were given a special pass.

Sean Fernandez gazed at Sheena and he thought just how attractive she was.

She was slim and tall with lustrous raven hair that she pinned in a bun, her make- up was light. She was one of the most attractive women he had ever met.

He always felt curious as to what attracted her to the CBI but she did not volunteer any personal details about her life.

As far as he knew, she was divorced and single.

He knew her age to be thirty- three and he thought she was youthful in appearance. He at thirty- eight was tall, rugged looking and though not strictly handsome, he was definitely attractive. He had that cynical, knowing look that had its own charm.

He was aware he was attractive to women and had played the field a bit in his younger days. Sown some wild oats. But lately, he had sworn off all relationships after his recent break up with a lawyer, Bianca, whom he had been friendly with since the past two years.

Bianca had been a gutsy lady with a no nonsense approach to life. Her professional demeanour had attracted him when they had met at a party. But she wanted marriage and he knew his job was often so consuming, marriage was difficult. He also knew she had not wanted kids. Besides, she had a bit of a dominating streak that he had tolerated but where marriage was concerned, he had this lurking suspicion that she desired to wear the pants.

She was one of those women who would not mind if her hubby sat at home minding the kids while she got a chance to work outside the home. It would suit some men but not him.

He suspected this because she had once jokingly said so. But her eyes had been serious and watchful.

He had known then, marriage to her would never work. She was too headstrong and feminist for his taste.

He had nothing against headstrong and feminist ladies but they were not his idea of marriage material.

And so they had parted ways, rather bitterly, for she had turned venomous and accused him of playing with her emotions. The words creep and bastard were flung at him and he had been shocked at her venom.

He had decided not to involve himself in any romance at least not for a while.

He finally decided after a lot of soul searching that he wanted to marry but the lady had to be so right that he would just never hesitate to tie the knot. Perhaps somewhere out there was that special lady awaiting him *if* he believed in fairy-tales. The truth was in his job it was hard to believe in fairy-tales. It was easier to believe in nightmares and monsters that lurked in the dark.

Then finally the plane took off. The air hostesses came around, smiling sweetly, their immaculately made up faces a sight for sore eyes. Sheena was seated beside him. If she was aware of his scrutiny, she gave no inkling of it. Her face was cool and composed. It was really hard to know just what went on in that mind of hers.

He wanted to tell her that she was beautiful but also knew that sexual harassment was frowned upon in their line of work. Any sexist remarks were construed as sexual harassment and an officer could be severely reprimanded if a complaint was made against him.

Thus, he busied himself pulling out a file and studying it intently. The slim file contained all relevant information about the case.

The plane landed in a few hours at Mumbai's Chhatrapati Shivaji International airport.

They were met at the airport by a car with a driver who took them along to the guest house.

Sean had been to Mumbai on several occasions, mainly for work purposes.

He gazed at the busy traffic laden streets interestedly.

Sheena at his side was looking at her mobile.

The guest house was in Andheri, fortunately close to the concerned police station they would work with. The car halted and they both got out. It was a black sedan used primarily for company purposes.

The driver, Alok said, as he helped them to carry their bags to the guest house, "Sir, my name is Alok. I will be of service anytime you need me. This is my mobile number."

He gave Sean as well as Sheena his mobile number. They both saved it on their phones.

It was understood they would have ready transport to take them anywhere they chose for work purposes only.

The guest house was a big bungalow that had several rooms to accommodate CBI officers.

Both were given adjacent rooms for the guest house at present was unoccupied by anyone.

The caretaker, Ramesh Patel greeted them and opened the front doors for their rooms.

Sean looked at Sheena and drawled, "Let's unpack then we will meet in two hours for dinner."
Ramesh Patel interjected, "Sir, all your meals will be served by our kitchen in your rooms, no worry."

Sean looked at him and thanked him.

He watched as Ramesh Patel, a short balding man walked away. Then he said, "Look, I hate eating alone. Care to join me?"

Sheena stared at him and said pointedly, "I think today I will unpack, have a long bath and then join you. Is that okay? I feel gritty."

"Yeah, fine take your time. No hurry. We will eat, then talk about the case. Tomorrow morning we will visit Inspector Rane. He is expecting us."

Sheena nodded and they both went into their new accommodation.

As Sean stepped in, he was happy to note that it was a fair sized accommodation. The large room was divided into a small living room, a small bedroom with a double bed, and a cupboard. It had an attached large bathroom with a small bath tub and separate shower area. The accommodation was designed not for families but single people. However, a family could stay there too if really required. There was a divan in the living room to accommodate a guest.

It was well decorated with careful thought.

He liked the look of the place. He unpacked, placing his clothes and possessions in the cupboard. He always travelled minimally and his possessions took merely a single shelf.

He decided that perhaps he ought to shower.

He had a quick shower and then changed into a T shirt and blue fitting jeans. He shaved in the small bathroom mirror and felt he looked presentable.

Then, he went into the living room and switched on the big plasma television, using the remote control. He decided to relax and unwind. He rarely smoked but noticed there was a packet of cigarettes and an ash tray thoughtfully provided on the side table.

He lit a cigarette and smoked as he watched the news channel.

As usual it was highly depressing with bomb threats being made by extremist groups, sudden deaths of celebrities, suicide by a well- known television actor. So what was new? Sometimes the world really stank, he thought a bit cynically.

Then, glancing at the clock, he was surprised that two hours had fled. The time was now nine.

It had grown dark outside and he could hear the cawing of the crows on the huge pipal tree directly next to his window.

Then the door rapped.

He got to his feet and opened it.

It was Sheena, clad in cropped black trousers and a green fitting T shirt. He thought she looked hot. But his face retained a bland look. None of his thoughts were mirrored there.

He gestured, "Come on in. I guess they serve dinner late here."

She entered and sat down on the soft red sofa crossing her legs quite elegantly.

She always had a good posture and to him this always contributed to a woman's appeal.

"I guess dinner is served late here."

Just then there was a knock on the door.

He opened it and the caretaker, Ramesh Patel stood there with a long tray bearing a few dishes and two plates.

He looked surprised viewing Sheena inside but Sean said smoothly, "We shall dine at my place every day."

Ramesh nodded, though he had a speculative look on his face.

He also apologised, "The cook was ill and came late today. Usually dinner is served latest by seven-thirty. I am sorry about the delay. Tomorrow the cook's assistant, Mohan will come with your breakfast, lunch and dinner."

"No problem."

Ramesh entered and carefully laid the tray on the centre table.

He then left, saying, "The boy, Mohan will come at ten to collect the tray."

Then, Sean shut the door.

They both helped themselves generously to the three dishes. One was a plain boiled rice, the second was a mixed vegetable and the last dish was a chicken masala.

He knew Ramesh had been appraised that both were non- vegetarians by the Delhi office.

The food was not exactly gourmet stuff but reasonably good and edible.

There was in a small covered bowl some *gajar halwa* which was a tasty carrot sweet laced with raisins and nuts.

Sean declined it but Sheena decided to have it.
Sean felt surprised for most women he knew dieted endlessly at least those that were as slim and well- proportioned as Sheena.

But Sheena said with a shrug, "You only live once, so when the opportunity presents itself like right now, I never say no."

"Good philosophy." Sean grinned.

His grin made him look devastatingly attractive as one old flame had once commented for Sheena stared at him, then looked hastily away.

After the dinner, Sean said, "Let's discuss the case."

Ch 3

Sheena nodded, all ears.

Sean took out the file from his small duffel bag.

He opened it and said, "I want you to read this tonight. I will give it to you. It was for both of us. But to surmise the case- Simran Chawla was crowned Miss India. The whole country celebrated at least Mumbai did. There were parties and tons of media exposure. She presented a happy, smiling facade to the media and every young woman longed to be in her shoes. At least most would. But just a few months later, her body was discovered on the street, directly in front of her building. She had apparently committed suicide from her home, the eighteenth floor, late afternoon around three- thirty or so. It was a long drop and the body was discovered by the passers-by at four that Wednesday afternoon, the 23rd of January. The police at Andheri investigated but could not find answers. There was no suicide note. Nobody understood it though apparently according to her parents she had emotional issues. She was seeing a counsellor for the past two years. Well, it should have been clear that since it was suicide, the case was solved. However, her parents have refused to accept it and approached the CBI themselves to look into the matter. Her dad has contacts with the State government and this has helped push it in their favour. So here we are, trying to figure out whether this really was a suicide or foul play."

Sheena listened and said, "Yes, I know this because I read all the news reports of it. God knows the internet is jammed with you tube videos of this case. Lots of speculations but no answers. The web sleuths are convinced it was murder. They post on the comment sections about who could have done it. But those are not facts just theories."

"And we deal with facts. So tomorrow morning, we go down to the police station and meet Inspector Rane. I do not know him personally for he has been transferred here only last year. I guess the poor guy is tearing his hair out in frustration. So we step in and help."

Sheena smiled and glanced at her silver wrist- watch, "It's eleven already. Past my bedtime. Better make a move and catch some shut eye."

Sean nodded.

She stood up gracefully and moved towards the door.

At the door he wished, "Goodnight, sweet dreams."

She turned back and looked at him, "You too."

Then, after he had seen her enter her accommodation and shut her door, only then he shut his own door and decided to catch some sleep. Tomorrow was going to be a long day.

Ch 4

 Sean phoned Alok at seven telling him they needed him to drive them to the Andheri police station.

Alok instantly agreed and told him he would be waiting at the entrance.

The breakfast was served by Mohan at quarter to eight. He was a smiling youth, ready to please.

At eight, Sheena knocked on his door. They both had a light breakfast of a bowl of cornflakes and three dosas with green chutney.

There was some tea too.

"That was nice!" Sean said happily, setting down his small empty tea cup.

Sheena agreed, "Will have to watch my weight here though."

Sean's eyes travelled over her lovely figure but he looked away for he knew the rules- staff members had to maintain a certain respectful distance and fraternising with female officers meant one had to be careful never to make a pass for if reported he could be in a soup.

Together they made their way to the waiting vehicle parked outside.

Alok greeted them deferentially.

He drove carefully, weaving through the heavy traffic for it was peak hour and office commuters were rushing to work.

"Give me the countryside sometimes." Sheena commented reflectively.

Sean looked at her, feeling surprised, "I pinned you down as a city girl."

"You would be surprised." Sheena drawled and looked away at his searching gaze.

She found him attractive but knew getting involved with him was playing with fire.

It was putting her job in jeopardy for one and two after her divorce, she was not keen on getting romantically involved with any man. She just wanted to concentrate on her job. Men did it all the time, well, so would she try to do it.

They reached the police station fifteen minutes later.

Both were directed to the office of Inspector Rane.

Inspector Rane sat behind his desk, his posture ramrod straight. He looked like an intelligent man and had a stern look on his face.

They were greeted politely, although a bit reservedly.

Sean sensed a bit of antagonism for he knew their presence here was confirmation that the police were not successful at solving the case.

But Sean had lots of charm. It was one of his traits that always stood him in good stead.

He was very polite and soon Inspector Rane had thawed a bit.

Sheena knew her presence also thawed the Inspector for he seemed to like the look of her. There was a look of admiration in his eyes when he glanced at her. Sheena suspected the stern Inspector liked attractive women. But didn't all the men?

Inspector Rane began talking, "The young lady was found sprawled on the street. It was a terrible sight. Fortunately no passers-by were hurt with the heavy impact as you know can happen."

Inspector Rane paused then continued, "The forensic pathologist gave us his report."

He fished through his file and handed it to both of them.

The autopsy report was short. It stated that the deceased Simran Chawla aged twenty, was five feet nine inches tall and weighed a hundred and twenty pounds. She had no distinguishing marks on her body. There were no scars or birthmarks. Death was instant.

Her stomach contents revealed she had had a light breakfast of muesli and milk and two bananas. There were also three sleeping tablets found in her body. In an orange fruit juice the tablets had been dissolved. It was clear that she had committed suicide before she fell asleep being most likely in a disoriented state.

Sean gave back the autopsy report,

Inspector Rane said, "We have not leaked this news of sleeping tablets being found in her system. We have decided to keep this case more private because the news hounds are having a field day calling us inept." His face had tightened.

Sean said sympathetically, "Yeah, those blood hounds are awful."

There was a moment of silence as Inspector Rane's face brightened a bit as if he sensed a sympathetic ally.

Sean asked, "What about her personal life?"

Inspector Rane said, "Well, she had a boyfriend, expected of course. She had one best friend and also a manager. "

"So basically on the day she died she had no visitors?"

 Inspector Rane frowned, "Of course, we examined that angle. Oddly enough all three of them paid her a visit that day. But unfortunately, also the CCTV cameras were not working that day because of some malfunction and they had been sent for servicing. Convenient if you ask me but this happens. It is hard to say if she had any other visitors."

Sean thought for a moment, "I see. So basically we may have three main suspects- the boyfriend, the best friend and the manager."

Inspector Rane nodded his head, "Yes, looks like that but all three were taken in for questioning. They all had good reasons for visiting her that day and in all appearances none had any real motive to see her dead. I think frankly, it is a case of suicide but her parents and the public cannot accept it. I mean the lady had it all- looks, fame and she would participate in the forthcoming Miss Universe later that year. Hardly the reason to commit suicide, yet who knows? Lots of these type of women are unbalanced. I mean in public they smile a lot but in private it's a pathetic sob story with counselling helping them cope with their tough hard lives." His tone was sarcastic.

Sheena asked, "So she was seeing a counsellor?"

Inspector Rane nodded, "Yes. She was seeing a counsellor who was attached to the St Mary's hospital which was a stone throw away from her residence. The counsellor's name..." He consulted his file and his face cleared, "Yes, Mrs Premilla Pandey. A lady who has practiced there for the last ten years. I interviewed her and all she said was that all records were confidential."

"I pointed out that if she cooperated with us, we could solve the case so she relented a bit. She showed us the report she had made on the deceased and it appears that the lady suffered from anxiety and depression. She had been on medication previously but right now all she did was to see a counsellor which she claimed helped her more than medication. At least that is what Mrs Premilla Pandey says. "

Sean pursed his lips, "I can see why it is a tough case."

Inspector Rane said, "We will be happy to assist you both in any way. You have our full co-operation. We want this to be solved. And believe me, I know it is suicide but we have to please the public."

"Yes, so we have stepped in." Sean said smoothly.

Inspector Rane gave him the addresses and mobiles of all the characters of the case.

There was nothing more to discuss because just then Inspector Rane received a phone call on his mobile from his superior.

Sean and Sheena took their leave.

Ch 5

As they stepped into the bright sunshine, Sean said, "Let's pay a visit to each of these characters. I think we will learn more. We will begin with Premilla Pandey."

Sheena agreed.

Alok drove them to St Mary's hospital.

Sean spoke on the mobile to Premilla Pandey.

Apparently, at the hour she had no clients and she told him that she would see him.

The hospital had been newly painted. The floors gleamed with white marble and it had the usual antiseptic hospital atmosphere with its harsh white fluorescent lights and serious faces all around.

"Depressing, isn't it? Sean said as they strode along the long corridors.

Sheena nodded, "Yes, definitely."

Mrs Premilla's office was on the second floor which they reached by lift. There was a smiling plump receptionist outside, who ushered them in.

The office was small and quite sterile looking. However, her desk had a few silver framed photographs that lent a homelier atmosphere to the place.

Mrs Premilla Pandey was a middle- aged lady, clad in a green sari, her straight fine hair in a short blunt cut. She had spectacles and wore only the lightest touch of lipstick.

She smiled as they entered.

Quickly, they both introduced themselves.

Premilla Pandey bade them to be seated on the hard backed chairs opposite her.

They did so.

She was pleasantly plump and had a kind expression on her face.

Sean looked intently at her and liked what he saw.

But he knew nobody was above suspicion. He believed in the dictum-guilty till proved innocent and not innocent till proved guilty. It saved a lot of trouble in his eyes, of feeling shocked at the truth when it emerged.

Premilla Pandey asked, "Will you have some coffee?"

Sean wanted to refuse but Sheena quickly "Yes, please."

There was a coffee pot on the table and it held fresh coffee.

Premilla stood up and she walked to the small table and poured out two glasses from the tray of five glasses kept at a corner.

Then she handed them the coffee.

"My clients always feel relaxed when I do this. It is funny how tea or coffee makes people feel comfortable."

"True." Sean agreed.

They both sipped the hot coffee appreciatively.

Then Sean set down his glass and asked, "You seem like a very intelligent lady. Tell me, have you any idea why she would commit suicide? After all she confided in you."

Premilla Pandey shook her head, "No, not really. In fact, I felt because of these visits once a week, she was doing better. She seemed to be able to fight her feelings of anxiety and depression. I would never have believed she would take this drastic step."

She paused, "But the human mind is a delicate thing. One never really gets in to the head or soul of another person, if you understand what I mean. You can live with a person for years and then be surprised at an action of theirs. People are not machines which are right or wrong. So basically, there is no black or white. Just shades of grey for every human being. They are unique and not easy to decipher."

Both of the Inspectors listened in silence.

"You know, Inspector, I really liked Simran. She was a nice lady. Perhaps she was not very worldly wise. There was a certain naïve quality about her but we must not forget that she was very young. Only twenty. She had not seen much of the world but her beauty and vivacious personality were good for winning the Miss India title. She spoke eloquently and well. She was educated being a graduate in Humanities and also had decided to pursue a degree in graphic design later."

Sean asked, "Was her relationship with her boyfriend a happy one?"

Premilla considered carefully, "You know she often spoke about him. His name was Vivek Roy and I never met him personally ever. But with the news media, I viewed his photos on you tube. I guess he was good looking enough and it did appear that she was totally smitten by him. I think she wanted to marry him. Marriage was on her mind. But he had a temper. He would shout and yell but once he had even slapped her. But she forgave him because he had apologised profusely and she believed him. We all know one slap most often leads to another in the future. But she loved him. What can I say? I knew she loved him so I did not try to interfere with their relationship."

Sean asked, "So he could be angry enough to kill her?"

Premilla shrugged, "I never met him but yes, anything is possible. Men who fly into rages rarely make good partners. They may even murder. But I knew counselling her about this would be detrimental. She had begun to trust me and perhaps later, I would have counselled her about this. All this while, we were dealing with her anxiety and fits of depression. In other words helping her to battle her personal inner demons."
There was a bit of a lull in the conversation. They sat there quietly, reflecting on the choices women made that could lead to bad consequences.

Sheena said, "What about her best friend?"

Premilla smiled, "Yes, her name was Aditi Patel. She was a Maharashtrian young lady around twenty- one. Both the girls had been friendly since school days. Simran seemed to like her. I did not know much about her but Simran did tell me that Aditi always stood by her in good and bad times. She seemed to be a loyal friend. I think Simran was very fond of her."

Sean asked, "I heard Simran had a manager."

"Yes, his name I think was Sanjeev Shetty. He was a middle- aged man, a bachelor. I think he really was attracted to Simran and she was a bit wary of him. In fact, she told me that she wanted to get rid of him. She was so pretty that men found her very appealing. I think he fancied her and she sensed it. She did not like this because to her he was old enough to be her father."

"I see." Sean said reflectively.

Sheena asked, "What about her parents?"

"Her relationship with them was good. You see she was the only child and they doted on her. I think she had a good relationship with them."

The receptionist outside called up saying her client, Mrs Saldana was waiting for her appointment.

Sean and Sheena thanked her for her time and the information that they assured her would assist them well enough.

They both got to their feet.

Premilla smiled politely, her eyes now alighting on the client, Mrs Saldanha, a dour faced elderly woman walking to her door.

Ch 6

In the bright hot sunshine, they both walked to the car waiting for them.

Alok, was smoking a cigarette which he hastily stubbed on viewing them. He was directed by Sean to the address of Vivek Roy. He was quite a smooth good driver, an expert at weaving deftly through Mumbai's traffic.

Sean decided to pay Vivek's residence a visit. He knew he wanted to get a feel of the suspect even if he could not interview him. One's environment revealed facets of one's personality.

It was ten minutes later when they reached a tall high rise. The high rise looked posh and the cream and blue façade looked newly painted. It was obviously a residence for the wealthier strata of society. The two bored security guards at the gate looked at them with disinterest.

Sean was wearing casual clothes like Sheena. He did not want to arouse interest or curiosity.

He went up to the bald security guard who sat indolently on his chair while the thinner man walked to and fro, talking on his mobile.

"I want to visit Vivek Roy."

The name was obviously familiar to both for they stared at him.

"Is Roy sir expecting you?' The bald one queried.

"No, it's a surprise visit." Sean said smoothly.

The bald guard scratched his head and the thinner guard said quickly, "He lives on the tenth floor- 1001."

"Thanks, I guess he is in."

The bald guard peered at the parking lot and said, "His car is still there. He drives a white Mercedes so yes, you can go up there. Shall I phone by intercom and let him know you have arrived?"

Sean said, "No, I want to surprise him. We are old pals."

The two guards looked him over and decided he seemed okay. They waved him to enter and again looked a bit bored. Obviously, there was really no excitement around here.

Alok waited in the car patiently, signalling that he would park at the corner since there was a *No Parking* sign clearly written on the gate.

Together the duo made their way through the big cemented grounds, through the long marble floored lobby and used the high speed stainless steel lift. It took them swiftly to the tenth floor.

The door was an ornate white door with big potted plants at the entrance, more for show really.

Sean peered at the name plate and realised that the flat was in Vivek's name. It was not a rental flat. The guy obviously was loaded in all appearances. He pealed the doorbell.

After a few seconds, it was opened by a tired looking middle- aged maid with a disgruntled expression.

Sean asked if Mr Vivek Roy was at home. He gave her his calling card.

The maid looked at him suspiciously but told him to wait there and that she would check. Three minutes later, she came to the door and said, "Please come in and have a seat." She glanced at Sheena interestedly as she handed Sean his visiting card back.

The living room was plush and it looked as if an interior decorator had enjoyed spending Vivek Roy's cash to make it look glamorous.

There was a big fish tank at the corner where coloured fish swam about through the bubbles from a white nude stone figure of a little boy placed at the centre.

They heard footsteps.

Then a tall and handsome guy walked in.

He was lean yet muscular with the kind of appeal that women often found attractive. There was a slight predatory gleam in his eyes and one felt that he was a shrewd businessman. He shook hands with both of them after Sean introduced Inspector Sheena Rai to him.

His eyes settled curiously on Sheena as if he found it hard to believe that police women could be so feminine and attractive. Sheena met his stare equably.

Sean knew women in male dominated fields could at times be aggressive or defensive because they sensed chauvinism from almost everyone they met. Even women were not always sympathetic to them feeling deep down that only males made good police officers or detectives. He understood this well and he never treated female colleagues with anything but respect.

 Sheena could look very professional when she was at work while looking feminine and attractive too. Sean had glimpsed a softer side of her the previous night when she had let down her guard by relaxing in his company and smiling. But this morning, she had been a bit aloof as if trying her best to keep her distance from him.

Vivek Roy did not look uncomfortable. His good looks and wealth had lent him a certain self- confidence that made him look quite at ease. Of course knowing they were CBI police officers, he was not totally relaxed and on his guard.

Sean said, "You know of course, that we are investigating the death of Simran for her parents are unconvinced that she committed suicide."

Vivek Roy nodded, "Yeah, I know this. Simran's dad got a lot a pull. He is a top shot in a government office. Her mum is a homemaker and I know how cut up they are. Well, I am devastated too, even if I do not go around with a long face."

Sheena asked, "Do you think Simran committed suicide?"

Her question seemed to catch him by surprise. He took a moment to consider this, "Well, does it matter what I think? I mean she was……well… you want be to be truthful, right?"

They nodded.

He went on, "Well, she had a lot of issues, I mean anxiety, depression and she was seeing this counsellor from St Mary's hospital about it. So generally women like this are prone to committing suicide, right? So I would not say that she did not do it. I just do not know."

He hesitated, "Look, few days ago before she died, we had a fight. She was always insecure about other women. She was never convinced I really loved her. I told her that she was the only one but she accused me of having flings."

"Flings with who? Sean asked swiftly.

Vivek hesitated and then made a face, "Okay, I will come clean. I am a friendly kind of guy and chicks sometimes misread this. I had an assistant who was quite attractive. She had a bit of a crush on me and Simran realised it and so she accused me. She threatened to kill herself and I had great difficulty pacifying her. In fact, I was so angry that I slapped her. I apologised but I felt guilty about it. I know hitting chicks is wrong but....she goaded me too much. I could literally tear my hair out in frustration when she got in her insecure moods and I got a bit of a temper, so that hardly helps." He paused. His frank admission surprised them both.

He went on, "Also a few weeks before she died she accused me of having an affair with her best friend, Aditi Patel."

"Did you have an affair with Aditi?" Sheena asked.

He shook his head, "God no! I mean, I am not a heel to do such a thing. But Simran grew hysterical. In fact, I had to leave her flat because of the ruckus she made. She could be high strung, you know. Now all this might paint a not so great picture of her. But in reality…" His face had softened, "She was a gem. Kind and quite loving, especially to people with hard luck stories. She had a soft heart and I loved her for it. I am more of a practical business minded kind of guy but she was a nice thing. God! I miss her!"

His face suddenly lost its usual arrogant look and it crumpled a bit.

Sean looked at him searchingly. He had met many criminals who were good actors and thought he generally could spot a liar. But Vivek seemed genuine enough. Yet, his police cynicism was too ingrained to be fully convinced.

However, he maintained a bland expression.

Sheena said, "It's hard, I know but anything that you remember to help us will be welcome. Any small detail that can help us get a clearer picture."

Her warmer tone seemed to thaw him for he brightened up.

He said thoughtfully, "We spoke the day before she… she died. She seemed a bit tense. I hung up quickly because I sensed she wanted to pick a fight. I remember she said that we would meet during the weekend and discuss what was on her mind. She was a bit evasive though. I had no inkling what she wanted to discuss. But yeah, she never trusted me, I wonder if she trusted any guy completely. She was what she was though and I did love her very much. I could forgive her anything."

He looked away, his face working a bit with emotion. "I had visited her at nine that day but our meeting was brief, because a client wanted to meet me at ten and I had to leave. She seemed okay not depressed."

Sensing there was nothing further to get from him, they both decided to leave. Both of them had developed a code, to signal to each other when enough was enough. It was a look Sean darted at her with a slight nod. Sheena then never continued the interview. It was a tactic that worked well between them.

So they both mutually got to their feet, thanking him for his time and feedback.

He walked with them to the door.

"Call us anytime if you think of something important regarding the case. Every detail helps." Sean said, turning to look at him and noticing he looked a bit depressed.

"Yeah I guess. It's like those detective books, all clues however tiny are vital." Vivek managed a wan smile.

Sean nodded, feeling a bit surprised at his observation. He did not think Vivek enjoyed reading detective stories. He seemed like the kind of guy who read business magazines.

He said, "Something like that. Call us if you remember something. That will help."

Vivek nodded and shut the door behind them.

"So what do you think?' Sean asked, as they sat in the car, driven by Alok.

Sheena looked up from her mobile phone that she was flicking through.

"Well, he seems an honest guy."

Sean said thoughtfully, "Yes, I felt the same. But you never know. Guys like him who attract beauty queens could be slippery and very smart."

"Perhaps but what's our next move?"

"Our next stop is the manager. He sounds like a bit of a creep."

He directed Alok to the manager's office that was just fifteen minutes away.

"Let's pay the guy a surprise visit. In all likelihood, he will be there."

Alok knew the building for he said, "It's a well -known office building."

He pulled up ten minutes later, in front of a tall glass building.

It looked quite posh and there were two security guards outside.

They did not however question Sean and Sheena but let them pass through.

Sean guessed they looked respectable enough and besides the building held more than fifty offices, so it must be hard for the guards to know everyone on sight.

 A glance at the board in the lobby told them that Sanjeev Shetty's office was on the fourth floor.

The lift carried them swiftly to the fourth floor.

There were five small offices on each floor.

It was easy looking at the name plates to find Shetty's office. It had a glass frosted door.

Sean rapped on the door.

A minute later, it was opened by a tall, well-built distinguished looking man in his late fifties. According to the file he had been given by Inspector Rane, the man was fifty- six.

He looked a bit younger though, for he looked well- groomed and well preserved. His skin was relatively smooth and unlined. One got the feeling he took care over his personal appearance. His hair was too dark to be natural and Sean suspected he dyed it for there was not a grey strand visible.

Sean introduced himself and Sheena and flashed his badge.

Sanjeev Shetty looked a bit startled but he bade them to enter.

His office was medium sized and it looked neat and clean. Sanjeev had taken pains to give it an expensive air with the addition of a cream fluffy carpet on the floor, silver photos of sunsets and sunrises on the walls and the walls were papered with expensive looking grey wall paper. The original flooring of vitrified tiles were changed by him and now Italian pink marble was laid out, that shone spotlessly.

The office was air- conditioned with light lace curtains on the windows that overlooked the adjacent park.

"Nice place." Sean complimented, as Shetty bade them to be seated.

"Yeah, it cost me a bomb to renovate it but in my business, appearances matter." He seemed a bit self- deprecating.

Sean asked, "I guess you know the reason for our visit."

"No, not really because I thought the Simran Chawla suicide was an open and shut case."

"No, there are loop holes and we intend to get answers."

Shetty seemed surprised, "Are you telling me that it may not be suicide?"

His amazement was seemingly genuine. He stared at Sheena and seemed to find it hard to believe she really was a police officer, especially as she was clad in casual jeans and a black cropped top, her appearance attractive and youthful.

Sean shrugged, "Perhaps, perhaps not. But her parents want answers, so we are here."

Sanjeev Shetty said, "Parents can never accept suicide. They always think it is foul play."

Sean did not reply to that but merely asked him, "Can you tell us when you saw Simran Chawla the last time?"

Sanjeev Shetty had obviously been questioned before by Inspector Rane so he had the answer ready, "Actually I met her on the day that she died, that was the 23rd January at around eleven. I met her because she had summoned me to her place. "

He paused, "She wanted me to put more news about her in the social media. I advised her to agree to pose for the popular women magazines and also I would post a few you tube videos of her. A foreign makeup artist visiting Mumbai wanted to do a makeup tutorial on her for the viewers. I told her to agree. We would work on this together. She seemed happy enough. She knew publicity was good."

"I see. So it was a cordial meeting, then?" Sheena asked, in her cool tones.

Shetty looked at her and said, "Yes, a business meeting but cordial enough. If you mean did we fight, then no."

Sean cleared his throat, "This might be upsetting to you but I want a truthful answer. " He paused and looked at Shetty straight in the eye, "Tell me, how was your relationship with Simran? Was it strictly professional?"

At this, Shetty flushed. "Of course it was."

"Well, according to her counsellor, Simran felt you were…. well a bit too close for comfort and wanted more than just a business relationship." Sean said in a matter of fact tone.

Shetty looked affronted. He blustered, "What nonsense! Who told you this? That bloody counsellor? She is lying, Simran would never have said such a thing. We shared a very good relationship. I am shocked! This wrong! I demand an apology from that…..counsellor. Tarnishing my good respected name!"

Sean looked intently at him. He suspected that Shetty could be lying because the man was protesting a bit too much.

He did not pursue this line of enquiry because he knew it might be useless for Simran was not alive to tell her side of the story.

Instead he asked, "How long did you stay there?"

Shetty shot him a suspicious look as if suspecting Sean was trying go trip him up. He thought for a moment, then said a bit sullenly, "Around an hour or so."

"The surveillance cameras that day were out for servicing so can anybody corroborate your story?"

Shetty considered this carefully, "Let me think."

 Then he said, "I went back here to my office and ate my tiffin here because generally I carry tiffin which my maid prepares for me. Look, I have a microwave oven here at the corner and a small fridge."

Sean noticed the two items which were placed behind a small wooden screen at the far end.

"Okay but surely someone musty have seen you."

Shetty shook his head, "The security guards saw me but no one else. You can question them."

He spoke quite confidently.

Sean nodded, "Okay, so you came here. Is there anything you would like to tell me that might assist us in this case?"

Shetty thought for a long moment and shrugged, "Look, you know how women are…" His eyes darted to Sheena and he apologised, "With all respect ma'am do not feel upset but sorry to say women can be difficult at times especially these beauty queens and actresses. Right now I am handling a film actress and god knows is she a handful! The airs she gives herself! I have a real job dealing with irate film directors, trust me. But will the diva listen? No, she pouts, sulks and does exactly as she pleases, knowing damn well she is riding the crest of stardom, now. I say now because stardom is flimsy and it lasts only for a while." He named a popular film actress and Sheena looked surprised for she always liked the actress.

Shetty looked at her and said, "Yeah, these chicks are given lines and they spew it out on film but real life is not reel life. They are not their screen characters. Sometimes I wish they were!" He mopped his face with a clean handkerchief as if he was feeling stressed.

Sean asked, "So you are saying Simran was difficult?"

Shetty shook his head, "Now, I did not say that but yes, she could be moody and prone to anxiety. She was not a diva as yet in her behaviour. I always soothed her and made her feel good but there is only so much I can do. I guess her counsellor did the rest of the job but we were not successful, were we? She killed herself!"

Sheena said quietly, "But we do not think so, not yet anyway till we have investigated the case. She might have been murdered."

Shetty shrugged, "If you say so. But she was a nice thing. Who would murder her? It makes no difference, does it? She is dead, nothing can bring her back."

For a moment, he looked a bit depressed.

Sean decided nothing more could be obtained from him but he said, "We will be back if we have further questions."

Shetty nodded, "Come back anytime. I don't mind."

His eyes settled on Sheena lingeringly and it was clear, he thought she was attractive. At that moment both realised he had an eye for pretty girls. Simran probably was not imagining that he wanted more than a business relationship with her.

The two got to their feet and left.

Ch 8

"The next stop will be back to our accommodation. We will eat lunch and rest for a while. At five, we will try to meet Inspector Rane." Sean said, as he directed Alok to go back to the guest house.

At the guest house, they were greeted by the caretaker, Ramesh who said, "I will see that your lunch is delivered to your room." He looked at Sean as he spoke. He was quite conservative and would not address women unless necessary.

Both Sean and Sheena went into his accommodation.

They sat together while Sean switched on the big plasma television to the news channel.

There was a pretty newsreader who was reading the latest news which featured the usual dismal news. But a few minutes later both of them leant forward unconsciously as the news reader announced the latest developments in the case of Simran Chawla. On screen there was footage of a pretty Simran being crowned Miss India, her smiling pretty face beaming as camera lights flashed around her. She looked poised and very self-confident. It was hard to believe she could ever suffer from the normal anxieties and melancholy of normal people yet she probably suffered more because she had sought counselling.

Human beings were hard to fathom, Sean thought. They presented one façade and their inner life reflected another story altogether.

The truth emerged only when tragedy struck.

Then, there flashed a footage of a slim, bearded news reporter who announced how devastated the parents were and that apparently the police were not making much progress. He also announced that the CBI was taking on the investigation, making not too subtle hints about the ineptitude of the current police at Andheri.

Then the next headline was about some hunger march by farmers in Bhopal.

There was a rap on the door.

Sean opened it and a smiling Mohan entered, bearing the silver tray. He set the tray down carefully on the centre table and then he left with a shy smile.

The meal was reasonably good. For dessert there were two pieces of chocolate burfi. Sean helped himself to both the pieces while Sheena refused saying she had better watch her weight.

After the meal, Sean took out his personal file. He made a few brief notes about the interviews they had conducted. They had taped every interview using the secret microphone taped to his chest. Sean always carried with him a microphone when he conducted interviews with witnesses or suspects. He never told the subjects that they were being taped because it put them too much on their guard. In many states this was allowed as admissible evidence.

They both made notes in the file taking turns to put in every important detail.

Then, Sean began to discuss the case, "Tell me what your opinion on Sanjeev Shetty is?"

Sheena shrugged, "He seems okay but I think Simran could not have imagined that he wanted more than just a professional relationship with her. Women have this gut instinct that is not often wrong. I think he may be a bit of a slippery character. He should top on our lists of suspects."

"Ah, but you forget the boyfriend, Vivek Roy. You are aware that in most murder cases, the spouse or the romantic partner is the first on top of the list of suspects and in more than fifty percent of homicides they are the perpetrator. So we cannot dismiss him."

"I think besides meeting Aditi Patel, we ought to meet the parents. They might provide good insight into the case, maybe we can see it from a different angle." Simran suggested.

Sean agreed, "Good idea. We will try to meet all of them tomorrow."

Thus, with that decision, they both decided to have a quick rest and then they would meet Inspector Rane at five because he wanted to speak to them. The meeting with Aditi would be later.

Sheena left for her room and Sean grabbed a quick nap on the divan.

Ch 9

At five, they were at the police station.

Inspector Rane greeted them with his usual reserve but this time he was more relaxed.

Sean told him about the interviews and played the recorder for him.

Inspector Rane listened carefully.

He said, "Now you see what we are against? Everyone seems innocent and yet the parents remain unconvinced. I sure as hell hope we are not barking up the wrong tree. But whatever the outcome, at least the public will be happy and satisfied."

He thrust the newspaper write up on page two of the Times of India. In it was a rather scathing piece of journalism about the police's ineptness and callous indifferent treatment of the case of the beauty queen, Simran Chawla.

The journalist went on to say that it was not possible for a young lady with such a good future to commit suicide. The journalist went on to cite quotes from relatives and colleagues who said she seemed happy and it was hard to believe she could take her life. So far it appeared that the police had not informed the public about her counselling visits for her depression and anxiety.

"We should put that out there but have decided not to because the parents want this to be kept confidential. They have begged me not to disclose her mental health issues to the public. So now we come across as the bad guys. Nice!"

He looked angry.

Sean pacified him, "The media and public always do this when there are no easy answers. They glorify these beauty queens and celebrities, putting them up on lofty pedestals and cannot believe they can have bad times or mental problems. It's just a fact of life."

Inspector Rane nodded, but he looked less angry now.

Sean somehow soothed him and Inspector Rane found himself taking a bit of a liking to the younger man. Sean had charm that was not too obvious but it always worked.

Sheena asked, "Will the parent's consent to an interview by us?"

"Yes, of course. I will contact them and let them know that you want to meet them today. Can you tell me the time you want to meet them? These older people generally do not like surprises. Besides they are so overwrought, I think it is best not to give them a surprise visit."

Sean said, "Perhaps in an hour's time if possible?"

Inspector Rane nodded and reached for his mobile.

The parents were at home and agreed to a meeting at their residence.

"We will also meet Aditi Patel but I think a surprise visit might be good." Sheena stated.

Inspector Rane agreed.

They left the police station and then decided to do a little exploring of Andheri before the scheduled visit to Simran's parents.

Alok was happy to drive them saying, "The points of interest here are several. For example the Funky Monkey's Play Centre and the Swami Samarath Temple. You have the Lokhandwala market, the Sri Radha Rasabihari Temple, the Mahakali cavers. There are more of course, if you want I can drive you around when you are free. Right now we will pass the Swami Samarath Temple in Lokhandwala. It is a nice tourist attraction."

He drove for fifteen minutes and then halted next to a beautiful crafted temple designed in a lotus which was the national flower of India. It was quite crowded and many people thronged there especially in the evenings.

Both of them clicked pictures on their mobiles.

Alok said, "I went in once. I could pray there because despite all the activity around here, the temple offers peace and quiet. Once inside, there is peace and serenity. Would you like to go in?"

But both refused politely saying, "Another time." It was now six o'clock and the interview with Simran's parents was scheduled for six- thirty. They might as well leave now.

Ch 10

The Chawla's resided in a small green and white building with three floors.

There was no ground floor since it was built on a height.

They resided on the last floor. There were no lifts and though it was not an expensive looking residential place, it was neat and clean.

Sean was a bit surprised for he had expected a posh looking residence.

They climbed the granite stairs to the third floor.

"If I lived here some of my exercise worries would be solved." Sheena stated with a wry smile.

"Yeah." Sean nodded.

There were just two flats per floor.

The Chawlas were at the left end. There was a gold name plate on the polished front door bearing their name- *The Chawlas.*

Sean rang the doorbell.

He heard some voices and then almost immediately the door was opened by a young maid who smiled and ushered them in as if she expected them.

They walked in and it was a small living room with an open kitchen. The open kitchen gave the living room a look of space.

Then, there were footsteps as a middle-aged couple walked in.

Mr Chawla was a stout tall balding man with a slightly protruding tummy and his wife was a slim lady who was rather tall.

She had an air of grace and poise about her. In looks, she was startlingly similar to her daughter, except that time had not be too kind to her for there were wrinkles on her face and her hair was flecked with grey.

Once seated, the introductions were made. The Chawla's expressed their happiness that the case was now in the CBI's hands.

"We want justice and the truth for our daughter."

The mother's eyes welled with tears, "She was our only child. We are all alone now."

Mr Chawla patted her hand comfortingly, "There, there! It is hard but we must answer these detectives without giving into emotion. We must assist them as much as we can."

His firm, but kind voice had the desired effect. His wife calmed down and gently dabbed her eyes with the end of her sari.

Sheen felt touched although she schooled her expression. It was never easy losing a child let alone an only child.

It had been decided by them that Sheena should try and talk to the mother who might feel more relaxed in a lady's company.

So Sheena asked, "Why were you both so sure that Simran your child would not have taken her own life? Surely you must have valid reasons."

Mrs Chawla sniffed and said, "I know my child. Maybe she was prone to anxiety and at times depression but she really was a nice and sensible young lady. She had just been crowned and the day before her…her death…" She swallowed hard and then continued after her husband patted her arm gently, "Well, she had told me that she was feeling better these days. The counselling had helped and she was feeling fine. Now naturally, I was happy. So you can imagine my shock on hearing the very next day, she committed suicide. I could not believe it and still cannot believe it."

Sheena said, "I understand but people can change moods from day to day also."

"Yes, but I am telling you that she did not commit suicide." Mrs Chawla's voice rose and Sean stepped in saying soothingly, "Yes, we believe you, Mrs Chawla but my colleague here is just trying to point out that these things happen. You see we have dealt in the past with suicide cases where the victim was actually in a jolly mood even a few hours before and then commits suicide. The human mind is a very complex mechanism. So please do not take offence."

Mr Chawla said quietly, "You must excuse my wife. She is just emotional. I know these things happen. Life is uncertain. But yet Simran may have been a bit …well… moody but she was not some mental case. She just had a few issues. She was not diagnosed as bi polar or suffering from paranoia or manic depression. She just had anxiety issues mainly and feelings of melancholy."

His voice lowered, "You see, Simran was a bit of a high achiever. Even at school she wanted to be in the top five and worked immensely hard and often enough reached her goals. The same at college. She wanted to achieve much and while we were not very much in favour of her entering the Miss India contest, she was adamant. She had done some modelling in college and liked it. She had told us that she loved modelling and hoped one day to become an actress but also that she would pursue a professional degree in case it did not work out. So we permitted her to take part and…. well… this is one decision we regret. Maybe the pressure was too much for her but she was gradually feeling more stable because she seemed happier. I just know she would not take her life. The previous week she told me her dream was to win the Miss Universe contest. She was… well…a high achiever and always determined to succeed at anything she liked. She had won singing competitions at school."

Mrs Chawla sniffed.

Sheena felt a bit uncomfortable at this display of emotion and felt herself feeling a bit emotional. They had been trained to be professionals and not give into emotions easily. It was an important part of the job. A police officer who went hysterical at every crime scene or got emotional about the victims could not then perform as an impartial, unprejudiced investigator.

She asked, "Can you tell us about her relationship with Vivek Roy?"

The couple looked at each other and as if cue, Mrs Chawla said, "Well, they had met a few years ago. Actually she had met him at a party. They got along well, began seeing each other and she fell in love with him. I think she was happy enough but I also knew that Vivek had a temper. His anger frightened her and once he had slapped her. I was angry to hear this and warned her about him for no man should hit a woman. One slap leads to another. But she felt it would never happen again. She really loved him. I understood that- I mean he was rich, doing well in his business of manufacturing garments and he was handsome. But I had my reservations and told her so."

Sean looked at Mr Chawla and asked, "Tell us, if you suspect anyone of being responsible for your daughter's death?'

Mr Chawla said, "She was beautiful, now famous and attracted tons of attention. She had no female friends except for Aditi but lately I think she and Aditi were not so pally with each other. I know this because I asked her to call Aditi to our place for lunch one Sunday afternoon when Simran wanted to visit us but she changed the topic and said she would come alone. I sensed she was no longer that friendly with Aditi. So you see, she was quite lonely and anyone could have been envious enough to harm her. I know her life seemed great on the surface but then all that glitters is not gold. She had her problems but not so severe she would kill herself. In many ways she could be level headed like that."

"So there were no stalkers or any guy who seemed harmful to her?"

Mr Chawla thought then said slowly, "Actually after she won the Miss India contest there were stalkers who phoned here trying to chat with her. There was one persistent guy named Varun Gupta who was very irritating. I almost changed our home phone number because of him. We always had a telephone at home but lately my wife bought a mobile for herself and got rid of the home telephone. I mean nowadays everyone has mobiles, telephones are too old fashioned, right? But the calls stopped after her death."

"Any idea who this guy may be?"

"Yes, I think he was a boy in her college because when I told her his name she only laughed and said Varun Gupta always had a crush on her and that he was harmless."

Sean said, "Any idea about his address?"

Mrs Chawla said, "He is on Facebook. Easy to find him because I saw his profile once to find out who he was. He stated that he went to St Xavier's college. He lives in Andheri too. But his actual address I have no idea about. He really was the limit!"

Sean said, "We will look into this too. Now, I think it is better both of you take our numbers because in case you need to talk to us, we can be reached."

After the couple had saved both the officer's numbers on their phone, Sean and Sheena took their leave.

Ch 11

On their way to Aditi Patel's residence, Sean said, "The couple seem nice people. I don't think they deserve what happened."

Sheena shrugged, "Life can be a bitch!"

"Yeah!" Sean agreed.

The car halted in front of a small three storied building that looked badly in need of a paint job. The plaster was peeling on some walls and the garden though small was filled with weeds and had absolutely no symmetry. The tiled path that led to the entrance was also shoddy for a few tiles were chipped and few were broken.

This surprised the detectives for they expected Aditi Patel to live in better surroundings.

According to the fat lazy looking security guard, chewing paan, posted at the front entrance, Aditi Patel had just arrived home from a trip to the market.

Apparently, she resided on the second floor.

There was no lift and both trudged up the stairs.

"Good!" Sheena said, "I am getting all the exercise I need."

Sean laughed, "So am I. Anymore of this and I will definitely eat all tonight's dessert. Nothing for you." They both laughed, feeling comfortable with each other. These past few days had drawn them close for the wall of reserve that Sheena had erected was crumbling down a bit.

There were two flats on each floor.

 It was easy to find her door for there was a large nameplate in gold lettering with the name *Aditi Pate*l on the rather faded surface.

Sean rang the doorbell.

There was no answer, so he rang it again after a few minutes.

Finally the door was opened.

Aditi Patel dressed in black jeans and a black T shirt stood at the threshold. She looked inquiringly at them.

Sean introduced both of them showing his badge and credentials.

Aditi said slowly, "I see. I heard that the CBI was tackling the case so I guess it's you guys."

She gestured, "Come on in. Don't mind the mess but my home is always like this. I like it this way." There was a look of defiance on her young face. Sean knew from the case file, Aditi was twenty- one years old. She looked a bit older though.

The living room was in a mess with books strewn on the floor and there was a pile of clothes dumped carelessly on two chairs. The paint on the walls was faded and in some corners it was peeling off. There was a small desk that was literally littered with papers, pens and books.

Whatever Aditi was she was honest enough to admit she was an untidy person. She seemed quite comfortable sitting on the long slightly frayed sofa with the detectives opposite her seated on the divan.

"Can I offer you guys something?"

And before they could refuse, she jumped up, walked into the kitchen and emerged with a tray bearing two glasses of soft drinks.

They accepted it, especially since she had placed an ice cube in each. It was a hot, humid day and cool refreshments were welcome.

They sipped their drinks quickly, then Sean began the interview. It had been decided that Sean should first question her rather aggressively and if she seemed to get defensive, Sheena would take over. This was a common police tactic of playing bad guy first and then the other police officer would step in playing the good guy, wining over the trust of the suspect.

Sean began, his voice a bit accusing, "I heard from many sources that you had a fall out with Simran."

Aditi looked a bit surprised, her eyes widening. But she regained her composure quickly, shaking her head, "Nonsense! We were good friends, always had been, thick as thieves." She joined two fingers together in a gesture to show they had been the best of pals.

But Sean looked unconvinced. He said a bit aggressively, "But that is not what we heard. Simran was keeping her distance from you."

Aditi's eyes flashed. Her anger was evident now.

She said coldly, "I don't know who told you this pack of lies but rest assured Simran was always close to me. We…. we were like sisters."

"Her parents told us she had kept you at a distance. Surely they would not lie?"

Aditi said angrily, "They never thought I was good enough for her. I lost my parents two years ago and live alone by myself. I manage." She stated this proudly, "My aunt helps out because she stays on the first floor and she visits me often. But Simran's parents never cared for me because I was not rich. They like rich people. They are not so rich themselves but wanted their daughter to mix only with rich people. Snobs that's what they are." There was a look of contempt in her voice.

Sean did not relent being aggressive in his questioning, "So you blame them, I guess. Do you blame them for the death of their daughter?"

Aditi said, "Maybe, who knows? They wanted her to be a high achiever and she had so much anxiety. It's often the parent's fault encouraging their daughter to aim very high, so high she got depressed and anxious."

Then Aditi's face crumpled a bit and she began to cry, "I do not know why you are blaming me. It is not my fault. What did I do?"

Sean glanced at Sheena who quickly stepped in.

She walked towards the girl, drew up a chair and sat beside her, "Look, we are police officers. We just want you to tell us the truth. Do not cry. We are not accusing you."

Aditi calmed down a bit after this for Sheena spoke kindly.

Sheena asked gently, "You saw here, didn't you not on the day she was murdered?"

Aditi nodded, "Yes, I paid her a visit. It was around twelve or so. I went to say hello because she had not….."
Her voice trailed off.

Sheena asked, "Is it true that now that she was such a star she had no time for you?"

Aditi hesitated. Then she said sadly, "Yes, that is true. She had no time for me. She gave herself airs. I tried to reach out to her."

"So the visit at twelve was not a success?"

Aditi hesitated, then said, "Well…no. She was nice but she was not the same girl I knew."

"Were there any witnesses who saw you at that time?"

Aditi shook her head, "No, the watchman was there but I doubt he will remember me."

"Okay."

Sean now took over, "Have you any idea why she would commit suicide? I mean when you met her what was her frame of mind?'

Aditi bit her lip, "I think she was a bit depressed. I can gauge moods you know. I think she felt anxious and maybe that is why she took the drastic step."

"Okay. Anything more you would like to add?"

Aditi shook her head, "I know nothing more."

The interview concluded.

Then, the two of them stood up and told her that if she remembered anything that could help their case, she should contact them.

Sean gave her his mobile number that she saved on her phone.

The two left.

Ch 12

A day later

The next stop was to Varun Gupta's residence. They had scanned his face book profile and it appeared he resided in Andheri. It was not hard to get his address because they had contacted St Xavier's college and had obtained his address from the office there. This took time because they had to formally pay a visit to the principal and talk to him before he parted with information. He was adamant on seeing their credential first which they showed gladly.

The principal had said, "Varun Gupta was a bit of a dud, to be honest. He wasted much of his time chasing girls and fooling with his pals."

He gave them Varun's address saying, "I have no idea if he has changed his address but this is the only permanent address I have."

 Now, this morning, they decided to pay a visit to his residence. It was quite close to the Andheri police station, just a five minute drive away.

The tall grey tower looked expensive and the grounds were well maintained.

The smiling security guard waved them in after they explained they wanted to meet Varun Gupta.

They did not reveal that they were CBI officers. Generally they did so only if the guards posed a problem about entry in the building. The guard said helpfully, "Varun lives on the third floor."

With that information, they entered the building gate and the lift took them up. The brown wooden door with a small name plate that read simply- *Gupta's* was opened by an elderly lady in a sari.

Sean introduced both of them showing his badge. The lady looked worried, "Is something wrong? Is Varun in trouble?"

Sean explained that they only wanted to talk to Varun.

"My husband runs a garage and Varun my son is there. He is helping his father to run the garage."

She then proceeded to give them the address of the garage named, Gupta Garage.

She watched them leave with a worried expression on her face.

Sean and Sheena set off with Alok at the wheel to Gupta garage which was a stone throw away from the residence.

They found both father and son, working on a black Mercedes.

After Sean explained to the duo why he wanted to talk to Varun, his father grudgingly said, "Alright but I want to be present too."

He led the way to a small air- conditioned office. Varun walked slowly as if he was nervous.

They sat down on the chairs facing each other.

Sean began, "You and Simran Chawla were at St Xavier's college?"

Varun looked nervous as he said quietly, "Yes, I was two grades ahead of her though."

"Okay. Now tell me about your relationship with her."

"Relationship? There was nothing of that sort. I barely knew her well enough."

"Yet you had a crush on her." Sean pointed out.

Varun flushed, "If you saw her, it was natural. She was cute and I liked her. But that was all." He looked defensive.

His father looked at him searchingly, his face worried.

"Okay. Now what about when Simran was crowned Miss India? Did you take to contacting her?"

The young man looked away, his face twitching a bit.

"Tell them, son." His father urged him.

Varun looked at Sean and mumbled, "Okay, I will admit it. I phoned her home a couple of times. It was harmless. I mean we had been together at the same college, I wanted to congratulate her. No harm in that, is there?"

He looked very defensive.

Sheena asked, "But her parent's claim you phoned there so often, it was as if you were stalking her. You cannot deny this."

"Stalking her? Is that what they call it? I was just being friendly."

Sean said, "There is a difference between being friendly and being a nuisance. It was upsetting for both of them."

Varun looked away.

His father said, "The boy is young. He made a mistake."

His father looked worried.

Sean asked, "So that was all there was to it. You never went to meet Simran?"

"No, I mean I hoped for a glimpse of her and even passed her home but we never met after she was crowned. I swear."

"Stalking women is a criminal offense and I would advise you not to do this again." Sean admonished sternly.

Varun looked at his tennis shoes and mumbled, "Yeah, I was stupid, I guess. I would not do this again. But I never meant her harm."

He looked a bit apologetic.

Sean said, "Well, if we have more questions, we will contact you."

He stood up, leaving both father and son looking worriedly at each other.

Sheena followed him out.

Ch 13

That evening, they both enjoyed the dinner of Dal Amritsari which was a dish made up of chana dal and urad dal, some white rice and a chicken curry.

The dessert this time were milk pedas.

Sheena had just one, while Sean ate five quite happily all at one go.

Then, Mohan entered ten minutes later and took away the tray, his face smiling. After he had left, Sean asked Sheena, "So, any ideas about things? There seems to be no light at the end of the tunnel. I can comprehend why Inspector Rane thinks it might be suicide."

Sheena bit her lip, a habit she had when she was thinking deeply.

She said, "You know I was thinking. We never questioned the security guard at Simran's place. We ought to do so. He might remember something, particularly the time each of the suspects visited Simran."

Sean looked at her with a bit of admiration, "Bingo! That is something that I should have thought of. The security guard. He might remember something. We will go there tomorrow morning and talk to him."

'Yes." Sheena said.

She then, watched as Sean made a report on the day's activities. All this would be given shortly to their superior, Director General Verma by fax.

Then an hour later, after he had finished, Sheena read it.

She nodded, "All there, every detail."

Sean shut the file.

He stretched a bit and said, "I will call it a day. Feeling a bit tired."

"Me too." Sheena said.

Sean looked at her and felt the wave of attraction to her. She looked calm and poised. It was not as if her face had a poker, expressionless look. In fact her eyes were dark and expressive and she had a lively look on her face yet she was poised and rarely revealed her feelings especially of melancholy or anxiety. He guessed her police training was partly responsible. He wondered about her personal life. Did she still love her husband whom she was now divorced from? He wondered if she was really divorced but was not sure, many couples were separated too or just leading separate lives.

He wanted to question her but was afraid of crossing boundaries. Dangerous boundaries. It was not permitted to get involved with officers romantically or sexually. But there was no rule that they could not marry if they chose to. It sounded contradictory but that was the way it was. He guessed any involvement would have to be top secret.

He felt though a stirring for her that was desire- desire for a woman he had not felt in a long time. His work these days was his priority. Both Sheena and he had a good track record of solving cases and they had been nicknamed the Express Squad because of their many successes. They had worked together for three years now. They got along well together and often seemed in tune with each other.

Yet, what did he really know about her? She was an enigma despite working on cases together. She never revealed much about herself. All he knew was that she resided close to the CBI head office and so did he. Yet, their paths had rarely crossed except at work. Urban cities were concrete jungles, you often may never know who resided just a few yards away from you. This impersonality was something all city dwellers got so used to that even if their neighbour turned out to be Jack the Ripper, they might not be that surprised. One scarcely knew his neighbour well enough.

Sheena seemed to sense his gaze for she looked at him, and their eyes met. An awareness flashed between them but Sheena looked away.

Sean felt compelled to ask her a few questions. Curiosity killed the cat might be true but right now he threw caution to the winds. Perhaps it was the good meal and dessert or just a new mellow atmosphere right now but he had to know.

"Tell me a bit about yourself. Your marriage...."

Sheena stared at him and in her eyes he caught the flash of something. Anger?

But her voice was cool, "Do you really want to know? You never seem interested before."

Sean shrugged, "You know why. We are trained to be impersonal."

"So why now?"

"Why not now?" He countered boldly.

Sheena settled back comfortably but there was a tenseness to her mouth. He noticed this for he knew her expressions well enough.

She said, "My personal life is my own. You never tell me about yours. But okay, I will tell you a bit. But it stays within these walls, okay?"

"Hiding dark secrets, eh?' he teased, but his eyes were watchful and serious.

Sheena shot him a look that warned him not to push it. He knew she could be touchy when she chose to, so he decided to keep his mouth shut and just listen.

Sheena said, "I guess everyone knows I am divorced. It is on the records, right? But what they do not know is that Manish, my husband died two years ago of cancer, prostate cancer. He was someone I met at college and we fell in love. But his parents were against it because we belonged to different castes. They were the kind to consult horoscopes made by astrologers. The horoscope was bad and they warned him never to marry me or he would regret it. He went ahead and married me. They refused to attend the wedding. But things soured quickly when I told him I would never stop working at least till I had kids. He wanted me to give up my police job because of the long hours and danger involved. But I refused. Besides, he was now estranged from his family. There was tension between us and finally it got unbearable. We could not..." Her voice suddenly broke and she looked away, blinking back sudden tears.

He did not speak.

She went on, swallowing hard, "We could not live together without tension and quarrels, not big quarrels but you get the picture. The love had gone. I still cared but he just drifted away, not wanting to make any effort to be understanding. So we decided to get a divorce particularly after I had worked on the Delhi serial killer case, and had been shot. He was very cut up and thought I was mad wanting my career so badly. Luckily, the bullet only hit my leg and I got better soon but he could not take it. He told me either I gave it up or he would divorce me. So you know the rest. We divorced."

There was a long silence as both sat there quietly, sensing a bridge had been crossed in their relationship.

"Do you regret your decision?" Sean finally queried.

"Of course sometimes because I liked being married, it gave me a feeling of security. I lost my parents in my teens and was brought up by a spinster aunt, the sister of my dad. She was kind but…..it was not the same thing. I guess I just wanted to get married and have my own home. So I married at twenty- six and was attached to the local police station at that time. But two years later, I was approached by the previous Director, who told me he thought I had good potential and why don't I think of joining the CBI? This was after I cracked the case of the murder of an elderly lady rather quickly. So I joined but Manish was angry. He hated my job and its hours and danger. That I carried a gun at times frightened him. "

Sean said quietly, "Average everyday people find our job threatening, it's not abnormal because it's one that is different and has dangers. So do not blame him too much."

"Taking his side, huh?" She chided but her face was more relaxed now. It felt good unburdening herself. It had been ages since she had talked about it, in fact the only person had been her aunt. Her aunt though kind had disapproved and thought that she ought to have given up her career for her marriage. To a certain extent Sheena understood this point of view yet she could not tell her about the rift that had long begun because of his family's attitude towards their marriage. She knew her marriage had always been on shaky ground. And now here she was confiding in Sean of all people. He was a bachelor and she knew he was no saint. He had told her of having a few girlfriends but none of the relationships had been long lasting or worked out.

Sean said quietly, "I am not taking sides but I know our job can be hectic and causes problems in relationships. We seem married to our careers and this takes its inevitable toll. So I am not surprised. But the main thing is you have the courage to face life bravely and I admire you for it."

Sheena said, "The guilt tears me. You see, I understand Manish better now. He was traditional and wanted a stay at home wife. This is a nice thing for family life but it was not for me. I did not want kids till a few years passed and he wanted a family as soon as possible. He was a family oriented kind of man, I guess."

Sean asked curiously, "What about now? Suppose you fall in love, would you be willing to give up your career?"

Sheena said, "I don't know. But perhaps. I think having kids is nice, my biological clock is ticking. I am in my thirties now. I know if my husband asked me to, I would stay at home. Not like some martyr but because I want a good, happy family life. Besides, this job is what I like, yet day in and out, the awful things we see, the dangers of dealing with crazies, I have doubts. Real doubts that I want this till I retire. Are the victim's families any happier? Can all this bring the dead back to life?"

"True but what they need are answers and closure. But you are right, it might give legal justice but once the deed is done, you cannot bring the dead back. But we also tackle drugs, smuggling and that's great, right? We are doing society a favour."

Sheena said, "Director Verma's wife has separated from him. She wants a divorce. They have two grown up kids and she wants a divorce, it's hard to believe." Sheena said.

"Why?"

"Because you would think she is happy he is a big shot, but then with people one can never tell. I know he is a bit of a workaholic and she probably resents this. But I cannot blame him, the guy has tremendous responsibilities."

Sean said, "Yeah, he is a good guy."

There was a bit of silence after this.

Sheena stood up, not looking at him, "I think I will go back to my accommodation. It is getting late."

Sean stood up too.

Sheena turned to look at him. An awareness flashed between them and in his eyes, she caught the flicker of desire. She knew if she gave him the green light, he would sweep her in his arms and they would kiss, perhaps things might go further. But she resisted. She merely said, "Goodnight"

He nodded, watching her leave. Quietly, she shut the door behind her.

He stood there and then, he sighed. Things were getting complicated but Sheena showed admirable self- control and reserve. He knew she was attracted to him like he was to her but yet, she knew any involvement would be disastrous unless it was with marriage in mind. They were known as the, "Express Squad' and he hated to jeopardise a good thing.

Ch 14

The next morning, Director Verma contacted him on his mobile. He wanted both written and verbal updates. Sean spent close to twenty minutes filling him up on their progress.

Director Verma said grimly, "You are doing okay but no progress yet. I say step it up, will you both? I want this case solved quickly."

Sean said, "We are doing our best, sir."

"Well, then get on with it. I want results fast." His tone was a bit brusque.

And he switched off his mobile leaving, Sean staring at it.

Both Sean and Sheena decided to pay a visit to the security guard at Simran Chawla's building.

Alok drove them there.

Alok waited for them at a corner, lighting his cigarette and flicking through you tube videos on his mobile. In his job, patience was the key.

There were times he had to wait for hours on end, so he knew how to while away the long hours.

Sean and Sheena showed their badges to the surprised looking security guard. A slender man with a cheerful face, he seemed enthusiastic to be co-operative.

He told them to step into his small cabin at the corner and there they could talk.

His name was Raju Sharma and he told them he came from a village on the outskirts of Delhi.

Sean asked him, "'Do you recall Simran having visitors that day she died?"

Raju sighed, "Inspector Rane of the Andheri police also questioned me. I see so many people come and go. It is hard to remember. But that day I did not see Aditi Patel entering. I know her name because she had come here previously to meet Simran. As for the others I think I may have seen her manager but is hard to recall if it was really on that day. The CCTV cameras were not working. I do not have a fantastic memory, I admit."

"Aditi said she entered at twelve or so." Sheena supplied helpfully.

"Yes, I know but you see at eleven- forty or so, one of the residents called me to her home to complain about the noise the dog below her home was making. The dog barks a lot and this elderly lady gets wild with anger. So I went up to pacify her and meet the flat owner of the barking dog. Also during the afternoon at around the time, three- thirty, she supposedly committed suicide…"

"You said supposedly.' Sean butted in.

Raju nodded, "Yes, sir, I guess you police do not think it is suicide, right? Simran Chawla was a nice girl, she always smiled and talked nicely to me. I think she would not have taken her life. I mean, she was Miss India. Why would she? It makes no sense."

"Yes, but where were you that afternoon?"

"Well, sir, I received a phone call from my uncle. He lives close by. He had fallen down and fractured his leg and wanted me to take him to the hospital. I contacted the chairman of the building by mobile and he told me to go and help out but to return as soon as possible. I left at two o'clock and returned at five. I was shocked that Simran had committed suicide."

Raju also told them how Simran had helped him with money on one occasion when he had been short of it. "She gave me five hundred rupees, sir without questioning me. I returned it back but got the feeling that she would not have minded if I had not returned it. She had a good heart, sir. If truly it was foul play, I hope the perpetrator hangs for it." He stated a bit fiercely.

Sensing, they could get no more information, Sean decided to return to the car.

But Sheena impulsively said, "Let's just hang about here. We will go back to the scene of crime- her place and look around."

They had the keys to her flat in order to assist them in their investigation for Inspector Rane had a search warrant. They shared the same privileges.

Sean looked at her and agreed. He knew Sheena's ideas were often good after his experience of working with her. He rarely refuted her impulsive decisions.

Ch 15

They walked together to the lobby, taking the lift to Simran's flat.

They entered the flat with the keys Sean carried.

Fortunately, he had attached the key to his key chain of his accommodation and it was easy to keep secure since he was the type of person who rarely lost keys, in many ways he was meticulous about things.

The flat had a gloomy forlorn air about it. He supposed he was sensitive to atmosphere. It was sealed off till the case was solved. Even her parents were not permitted to enter without permission.

The flat was the scene of the crime though death had been on the street where she was found.

He went to the living room's open balcony which had no grills and knew that this was the balcony where she supposedly had jumped to her death. He looked down at the street down below and grimaced. It was quite a long drop. He tried to imagine how she must have felt while falling down but knew since her system had a few sleeping tablets, she must have been very groggy and perhaps it must have felt like a dream. Falling from heights in dreams was something he had experienced in the past especially during stressful periods of his life. So he conceded if she had been slightly drugged by the sleeping pills, to her falling must have had an unreal dream like feeling. Only this time she never awoke, just died.

He noticed the balcony had a low ledge in the centre and most of the flats around had put long fancy grills as a safety measure. Perhaps she liked the look of a balcony with no grills. The windows he noticed had grills but not this balcony.

It would have been relatively easy even for not a very strong person to lead her to the balcony and give her a shove. She had been slightly underweight. She would not have struggled much but been too sleepy to protest.

He gave an involuntary shudder at the scene. The barbaric things people committed. He had a strong gut feeling that this was precisely what had happened.

Sheena joined him for she had been walking around the two bedroom flat, moving from room to room.

"Easy, isn't it to get pushed? Why the hell did she not put grills?" Sheena peered down below and felt a bit dizzy. Heights always had that effect on her.

Sean shrugged, "The view from here is pretty good. You can see quite a good view of the city. She must have enjoyed sitting here having a cup of tea. She must have thought grills would ruin the open effect which it does but safety is more important, isn't it?"

They both noticed two chairs opposite each other with a small side- table against the right corner.

Both imagined the cosy tea drinking scene and Sheena said, "I found several packets of green and black tea in her kitchen cabinet. She was not a coffee drinker, not a jar of coffee in sight."

Sean said, "We have not checked her bedroom. Let's do that."

Together they walked into what seemed like Simran's bedroom.

The other bedroom at the far end seemed like a guest room for there was only a single divan and nothing else. Obviously Simran did not really use the room and perhaps had put off furnishing it for a later date.

Her bedroom had a double bed with a soft pink satin quilt. There were two teak cupboards, both had long full length mirrors. There was a small pink dressing table with an oval mirror, lit up with a two feet white tube-light. It had several cosmetics lined neatly.

They opened her cupboards and found piles of clothes. Some were neatly folded, others were hung on hangars.

There were two drawers in her cupboard.

It was filled with cosmetics like palettes of lipsticks, foundations, blushers etc. The other drawer had some notebooks and pens.

Sean took out the notebooks. In the first one there were many addresses and phone numbers. The second notebook was filled with recipes and beauty tips. He guessed Simran liked to jot down recipes and beauty tips. Cooking and beauty interested her like many normal young women.

He looked through it but found nothing of real interest.

Sheena read one of the beauty tips after he handed it over to her, "In order to make your lips look fuller, first line your lips with a darker lip pencil or lip crayon, then fill in with a lighter colour. The lightest portion should be the centre of your lips. Finish off with lip gloss or plain old Vaseline jelly. This was by Marilyn Monroe, the Hollywood actress."

Sean shrugged, "Girls will be girls."

There was a small side- table with a table lamp next to the bed. He found several fiction books on the table and in the drawer inside were boxes containing accessories like earrings and costume jewellery.

One got the impression that Simran Chawla was quite a neat person and liked to keep everything in its place. Quite the opposite from her best pal Aditi Patel, Sean thought.

There was a grey carpet on the floor. The room looked cosy and neat. He imagined Simran lying in bed and reading a novel with the table light on. The image was so clear to him, he was surprised.

On the wall opposite the bed hung a big poster of her posing for the camera with a crown on her head. She was wearing a beautiful slim fitting cream gown, her hair in an up do, her make up expertly applied. She was smiling and beaming, and she looked self- assured and poised. Hard to believe looking at that photo, she could have suffered frequently from depression and anxiety.

The attached bathroom had several glass shelves lined with expensive looking toiletries, ranging from face scrubs, shampoos, hair scrubs, hair oils, body lotions, and hair masques, both for face and hair. There were several soaps in soap dishes that were of the expensive type. There were few face washes too that were from expensive foreign brands.

Sean looked at her and murmured, "God! Do women need so much to look beautiful? Or is it just beauty queens?"

Sheena shrugged, "This is nothing. I visited the home of an actress once in my investigation and she had double this in her bathroom. I had looked at them and thought that if she ever got broke, she could start a small shop."

Sean laughed, "Women!"

Sheena countered, "That's chauvinistic! Men today are quite conscious of their looks. They too use cosmetics and toiletries."

Sean shuddered, "Count me out!"

"Oh, don't tell me you don't use anything." Sheena teased.

Sean made a face, "Okay, guilty! I use a coconut hair oil, and I use just plain bar soap for body and Johnson's baby shampoo for my hair. It's good enough for me. That's all."

Sheena smiled, "So you do take care."

"Cut it out! Sean rasped, pretending to look stern.

They both shared a good laugh.

It eased some of the tension of the case.

Both of them did not expect to find much here of interest in the way of clues because they knew Inspector Rane and his team had already gone through the apartment well enough.

But Sean knew he had to perform his duty thoroughly and leave no stone unturned.

They checked the second bedroom but other than the single divan, it was bare and empty. Even the blue tiled bathroom attached looked quite empty. There was a small cabinet but it was empty. There was just a half empty Dettol hand-wash inside. It was obvious that Simran rarely used the bathroom, at least not for bathing purposes.

The kitchen was the last room in the small flat which was around seven hundred feet carpet area.

It was small enough to accommodate only three people comfortably. It was a cream and grey modular kitchen which was neat and clean. The kitchen cabinets were stacked with rows of masala bottles and other culinary items like flour, desiccated coconut etc.

Sean knew Simran never cooked but had a daily cook woman come in. However, according to Inspector Rane on that day the maid had come in earlier than usual at around seven in the morning, cooked the meals and left. He knew this from the case file interview by Inspector Rane. She had to leave early because her son was sick in the hospital which was confirmed by the hospital records. So, Sean had decided not to pursue this line of inquiry because the maid was now working for Simran's parents and according to the parents she was quite a good decent lady.

They hovered around but found nothing of interest. The fridge was bare and had been cleaned by her parents with the permission of Inspector Rane who after examining the fridge and its meagre contents found nothing incriminating that could assist him in the investigation. According to his report, the fridge before being cleaned had a small tub of ice – cream that had been barely touched. There had been some eggs and a carton of fruit juice which had been unopened. An opened milk carton had been half full. The bottom tray had stored vegetables and fruits. The freezer had a few chicken packets and fish too.

Sean and Sheena decided that there seemed nothing of interest in the home.

Sean said, "Let's go. We could come here again but I think it's pointless."

Sheena agreed.

Ch 16

They both strode out of the flat and Sean locked it using the key.

Sheena stood by his side, waiting.

The opposite door was ajar. Sheena glancing to her left, glimpsed a young face staring at her and then the face vanished. She heard the click of the door being shut.

She frowned. Suddenly an idea sprang in her mind.

She walked to the opposite flat and rang the bell.

Seconds later, the door was opened by a young girl who seemed around twelve or so. She was thin, slight and had a bold expression on her face.

"Who is that?" A maid came into her line of vision.

Sheena looked at the girl and asked, "Is it okay if we talk to you for a few minutes?"

The maid intervened, "Who are you?"

Sheena showed her badge. The eyes of the young maid widened and she looked frightened. The lower classes always felt frightened when confronted by the police. They felt vulnerable as if they suspected they were suspects and jail was the place they would be put into.

But Sheena said quietly, "Nothing to worry but we only want to talk to this little girl."
The girl said, "I am not so little. I am twelve years old." Her eyes flashed a bit in annoyance.

Sheena hastily said, "Of course you are quite grown up, so can we come in?"

The girl hesitated but nodded, "Yes, I guess so. Come in."

The maid hovered in the living room and Sheena entered. Sean walked into the flat, looking a bit confused. He quirked a thick eyebrow at Sheena who just said, "Just chatting with this young lady."

The girl sat opposite them, stretching her jean clad legs and staring at both of them.

She now seemed a bit tongue- tied, looking a bit worried if the presence of cops was something unreal to her. Sheena could guess it probably was.

"Are you going to take me to the police station?" The girl questioned anxiously.

Sean reassured her, "Nothing like that."

She looked at Sean and seemed to be in awe of him for she blushed a bit and looked away shyly. Sheena adroitly took over, flashing Sean the look that said- *Let me handle this.*

Sean settled back and listened attentively.

The flat he noticed was almost a mirror image of Simran's but it was more simply furnished.

Sheena asked, "Where are your parents?"

The girl replied, "Both are working. Today I have a holiday to study for my upcoming exams next week. They will last for just a week. And then……" She grinned, "We will have our summer vacations. Boy! I am looking forward to them."

"Really? Planned some nice vacation?"

"Oh yes. My parents will take me to Chandigarh, where my grandparents live. We will be there for two weeks. They have a big house, you know, with a big garden. My grandfather was a botanist." She said this importantly.

Sheena nodded, "Nice. Now I did not get your name."

"Oh, yes. My name is Hema. You see my mother liked the Bollywood actress Hema Malini, so she decided to call me Hema."

"Kind of suits you." Sheena smiled.

Hema looked pleased.

Sheena said, "We are, as you know, police officers. I bet you never met police officers before."

"Right, you don't look like a cop." She stared at Sheena avidly and with great interest as if Sheena was an outer space specimen worth examining.

Sheena said, "I guess you know your neighbour Simran Chawla was crowned Miss India."

Hema perked up visibly, "Yes, that's kind of neat. I mean living next to Miss India. But…" She lowered her voice, "But she kind of kept to herself. I caught her once at her door without make up and I thought she looked nice but not…not you know like Miss India."

"You must have been sad when she died."

"Yes, totally shocked. It felt unreal. Whoever heard of Miss India killing herself after being crowned? I mean it was strange."

Hema stared at both of them. She seemed an intelligent girl. She also was a bit precocious for her age, despite her small build, "You are not convinced that it was suicide. I heard my parents talk about it while reading the newspapers. I guess you think it was….. What exactly is that word… foul…?"

"Foul play." Sheena said helpfully.

"Yes, murder to put it plainly." Hema said excitedly, "I knew it! I knew it had to be more than suicide. Neat!"

Sean raised his eyebrows. Today's kids were really a precocious bunch, they often said what they thought. He remembered his own youth, he had been quieter and reserved with elders than today's youth.

The maid tired of standing went into the kitchen. She emerged with two glasses of cool water. Both took the glasses for it was just a simple gesture of hospitality.

Sheena drank some of the water and then placed the glass on the centre table. She said conversationally, "Simran died on a Wednesday the 23rd January, do you remember that day?"

Hema screwed up her face and nodded, "Yeah, I remember."

"Really" You must have a good memory for days and dates."

Hema looked pleased, "Yes, I do, Mum says I have a very good memory. It is important you know to have a good memory, helps in exams. I bet cops need to have good memories too."

Sean cleared his throat, feeling amused. Sheena flashed him a warning look. He looked away and sipped the water.

Sheena agreed, "Yes, we too have to have good memories, maybe one day you might become a cop too."

Hema shook her head, "No way! I am going to become an aeronautical engineer." She looked very proud as she said this.

"Great!" Sheena knew this could go on forever because it was obvious Hema had quite an inflated opinion about herself, not in an obnoxious way though.

She seemed quite likeable too for she had a nice smile and had an endearing way about her.

Sheena asked, "On that day when Simran had died, were you at home or in school?"

Hema answered, "Well, I remember that day quite well because you see on that day it had been our talent contest in school. I had taken part in the poetry competition. I stood third." This was said in a pleased manner.

Sheena said, "Congrats! So you remember that day well, I guess especially since you have a good memory."

"Well, yes." Hema looked a bit wary now as if she sensed Sheena wanted something important from her but could not comprehend just what.

"You must have seen her body, right?"

"Well, yes, I heard some commotion from the people below. She was bloodied and kind of smashed, not like a potato chop but you get the drift."

"Yes, of course." Sheena said solemnly.

Hema inclined her head, as if waiting for more questions. She was very intelligent and sensed Sheena wanted more information.

Sheena sighed, "The problem is that nobody saw anyone visiting Simran that day. The CCTV cameras were not working and Simran had visitors but nobody saw them."

Hema frowned, "Yes the CCTV cameras were not working, I guess. I heard mum say that to dad in the morning of the suicide. I thought nothing of it. But yes, she had a visitor."

Sean sat up straighter.

Sheena said quietly, "So you saw visitors at her place."

Hema shook her heads, "Sorry, not *visitors.*"

Sheena looked disappointed, "But you said…"

Hema corrected knowledgeably, "You used the plural, visitors. I saw just one visitor."

Sheena leant forward unconsciously, "So you saw someone at her home that day. Was it the maid?"

"I know how her maid looks like. Wears a sari and is old. But this visitor was a guest, not a maid."

"Who was it and at what time?"

Hema regarded her curiously, "This is important, right? Like some kind of clue, right? I read a few detective books and clues are vital for the police. Is this a clue?"

Sheena said, "Maybe."

Hema nodded, "Okay, this is what I saw. I saw a young lady around Simran's age at her door. She had rung the bell and then Simran admitted her in."

Sheena asked, "How did you see her? Your door was open?"

Hema said gleefully, "No, through the peephole."

Sheena frowned.
Hema said, "Look, let me explain. You see that day, my mother rang up from her workplace that is the bank she works in and told me to go outside to check the letter box. The letter box is right outside our door."

"Yes, I saw it."

"Well, my mother was waiting for a wedding invitation to some cousin's wedding that had not arrived as yet. It was a wedding at Orissa, where this girl cousin resides. So my mother was anxious to receive it. She had rung me up and told me to check for her aunt told her that morning that since it had been posted she ought to receive it. I went to the door but heard sounds from the passage of footsteps. You know ladies like wearing heels and some shoes do make noise, click, click."

"Yes." Sheena nodded.

Sean looked a bit amused although he listened very attentively.

"Well, I looked through the peephole and I saw this young lady clad in jeans and a T shirt wearing these silly shoes and walking towards Simran's door. I watched her as she rang the bell and then Simran opened it."

"What time was this?"

"This was around three o' clock. I know because my maid brings me some snacks around this time to give me energy while I am studying. You know snacks like sandwiches or potato chips."

"Okay."

"So I saw her through the peephole and I did not see her leave though. I had been in my room studying. But one hour later, Simran died. "

"So you never saw this lady leave?"

"I said so just now, right?"

"Yes, you did. Could you identify the lady?"

"Well, I saw the back of her and three quarters of her face while she stood at the door. But yes, I may be able to."

Sheena looked at Sean who had photos in his mobile of all the suspects.

He passed it to Sheena who showed Hema a photo.

"Yes, that is her. I know it is. She was no glamour queen like Simran. I remember her long frizzy hair in a ponytail. Yes, it's her alright."

Sean took over, "So you are very sure, right?'

"Right." Hema nodded.

Sean had not been recording the interview. He now placed the recording device in front of Hema who stared at it.

"This is a recording device. I want you to speak to it and tell me what you saw in your own words one more time."

Hema said, "Wow! This is like some TV show. "

But she was game to talk and this she did well, quite articulate.

Then Sean said putting off the device for a moment, "The lady's name is Aditi Patel. Will you say that here for this recorder?"

Hema nodded. Sean pressed the button on again.

Hema stated, "I saw Aditi Patel at Simran Chawla's home at around three in the afternoon on the 23rd of January. She entered in the home but I did not see her leave. Then at four, an hour later, Simran committed suicide. I saw her dead body from my living room balcony. It was terrible!"

Hema looked up as Sean pressed the button off.

"Is that okay?"

It's great!" Sean praised. Then, they both stood up. Sheena asked,

"I guess you have nothing more to add, right? No more clues for us." Her voice had a slight teasing note that kids liked.

Hema though took it very seriously. She thought carefully for a long moment, then almost wistfully she murmured, "I liked Simran. I hope you get the killer and the killer hangs for it."

Both of them agreed solemnly and then let themselves out.

Ch 17

Inspector Rane was appraised of the developments in the case. He told them that a search warrant ought to be got to search the home of Aditi Patel.

It took them a few days but the search warrant was obtained from a judge named, Judge Patil, a renowned judge who had close ties with the

Director General Inspector Verma. At work the two men shared a formal relationship but informally they chatted on the phone once in a while.

A search warrant is a written order signed by a judge directing a law enforcement officer to conduct a search of a person or property. This search warrant was very important, for in searching the home of a suspect, many important pieces of information could be obtained that helped fit the pieces of the jigsaw puzzle more easily.

 It was a surprised Aditi who opened the door early morning, the very next day after the warrant had arrived. Clad in pyjamas and a white T shirt, she looked sleepy, her frizzy hair mussed up, her face shiny.

She was told firmly that her home would be searched. She protested loudly but Sean said coldly, "Ma'am, this is a legal order so please co-operate otherwise you could be behind bars for non- co-operation and obstruction of justice."

This he found generally worked with even the most hardened criminals.

Aditi kept quiet then and she let them enter. She sat in the living room nursing a cup of coffee, and looked tense and angry.

Sean and Sheena along with two constables went from room to room. There was nothing that was found to be really incriminating. But after fifteen minutes, Sean found a pair of fancy blue shoes that had heels. It was the only pair of shoes in the shoe rack that had heels and the rest were flats and sneakers. He bagged the shoes as evidence since Hema had told them that Aditi had worn heels the day she had last visited Simran.

However after half an hour, while searching the dressing table draws, Sheena found a letter. It was half- completed and tucked in a notebook containing addresses.

In it was a letter that surprised Sheena very much.

Silently she handed it over to Sean.

Sean read it carefully.

"This is it! We better take her down for questioning."

He pocketed the letter. Sean searched bathroom and found what he was looking for. He bagged it in the evidence bag carefully, showing his finding to Sheena.

He walked to the living room and told a mutinous angry looking Aditi, "You have to accompany us to the police station. Dress up. I am giving you ten minutes."

Aditi stood up, twin spots of colour on her cheeks, "This is outrageous! I want my lawyer. I refuse to be treated like a common criminal. I have done nothing! I am innocent!"

"You will have all you need in due time but for now please come with us."

He said this firmly but politely. She viewed the steel in his eyes and hesitated but just for a moment.

Then she walked into her bedroom. She shut the door.

Minutes later, she opened it and walked out clad in blue jeans and a red fitting shirt. She had tied her hair into a casual bun and her face looked freshly washed.

She said listlessly, "I am ready."

They walked out together, seated in the car driven by Alok to the Andheri Police station.

Ch 18

Aditi was the small interrogation room. It had three chairs and a small wooden table. There was a huge mirror on one wall that served as a two way mirror. Behind that mirror in the adjoining room stood Inspector Rane and Sub- Inspector Das who assisted him.

Aditi sat on one of the chairs with Sean and Sheena facing her.

After her rights had been quickly read, Sean began the interrogation.

Aditi denied having any involvement in Simran's death. She protested vehemently. She had a slight touch of arrogance in her manner. But this changed when Sean silently handed over the letter found in her flat.

She stared at it and her face looked frightened. It read,

Dear Vivek,

I love you very much. From the moment I saw you, I knew I loved you. Simran is a loser, she is mentally sick. You could never be happy with such a woman. I know we could be happy together. When we talk, I feel we understand each other.

I wish Simran was dead and we could be together. I know if she died, you would turn to me and I could comfort you. Our love could be a film story because we are made for each other. I consulted an astrologer and he told me that my true love was with a man whose initials were V and R. That is you, my dearest. Fate arranged for us to meet but that woman is in the way.

The letter ended abruptly as if Aditi had not intended it to be posted but just vented out her feelings.

Then Sean asked, "Is it true that you were in love with Vivek Roy?"

Aditi wanted to deny this but the half written letter was too incriminating.

She said sullenly, "I did not post the letter and being in love with anyone is not a crime."

"Well, try telling a judge who reads that letter and we will see."

Aditi's face paled. "I had nothing to do with Simran's death. I only met her at twelve that day of her suicide."

Sheena said quietly, "Actually we have a witness who saw you in the afternoon at three."

At this Aditi gave a start. She said, "Nonsense! No one saw me....."

Sheena said, "But you were seen at three ringing the doorbell of Simran Chawla. You were wearing jeans and your heeled shoes had a clicking sound to them. Am I right?"

Aditi looked at her, fear in her eyes. She had lost some of her composure.

Quietly Sean reached out from the bag under the desk and took out the pair of the two inch blue shoes, "We found these in your flat. You wore these shoes on that day." It was a wild guess and he was sure he was spot on.

Aditi looked at the shoes and suddenly she said, "I want a lawyer, I need a lawyer."

"All in good time. Now we are taking a break. We will be back." Both stood up.

They left the interrogation room and joined Inspector Rane watching in the adjoining room besides the two way mirror.

"So what do you think? Sean asked, his eyes on Aditi, sitting down, with her hands covering her face as if she was distraught.

"Guilty as sin. Keep her there for an hour. She will thaw, this works often enough."

Thus Aditi Patel, was kept in that solitary room for almost two hours. She was not given anything to eat, although there was a glass of water on the table. Yet it remained untouched. She just sat there, staring into space. At times she buried her head on the table and sat like that for a long time. It was obvious she was under great stress. Sean knew she would soon crack.

After two hours, Sean walked into the interrogation room.

He was now playing the bad cop. He said gruffly, "The evidence we have here is enough to put you in jail. So tell us what happened. Perhaps it was not your fault. Maybe she hurt you enough and you took revenge. Tell me, I want you to tell the truth what actually happened."

Aditi said, "I want my lawyer."

"Were you so madly in love with Vivek that you killed her? A nice girl like Simran, a good girl, a beautiful girl."

He was being provocative.

Aditi rose to this, saying, "Simran was a bitch!"

Ch 19

At that moment, Sheena walked in and sat beside Sean. She said sympathetically, "Yes, she may have been a bitch to you. Is that why you hate her?"

Aditi looked at Sheena and said mutinously, "I want my lawyer, I know my rights."

Sheena persisted in her nice cop manner, "You loved Vivek and Simran was in the way. It is understandable you harboured feelings of resentment."

Aditi said, "I hated her! Is that what you want to know? But that does not mean I killed her. You got no proof." There was a cunning look in her eyes, she was like a cornered rat doing her best to escape.

Sean played his final card. He laid a strip of tablets on the table. Three of them were missing, He said smoothly, "Here is the strip of sleeping tablets you administered to Simran. Three are missing. They were in your bathroom. No judge will believe you after this."

Aditi said, "These are my sleeping tablets. I use them at times."

"But these which are missing were given to drug Simran, were they not?"

Aditi just stared at him.

Sheena said quietly, "We found the glass you spiked with these sleeping tablets. Your fingerprints are on it."

This was untrue because the glasses at Simran's that both had drunk from had been washed carefully by Aditi after they had been used.

But she fell for it.

She said, "I need my lawyer. I may have drugged her but nothing more."

Sean pounced, "So you admit you drugged her."

Aditi looked away, refusing to speak.

Sheena said, "Look here, you were witnessed at her home at three. She fell to her death at four. You drugged her because you wanted her boyfriend Vivek for yourself. Now no jury will believe in your innocence. So come clean and tell us the truth. "

Aditi began to cry, her eyes filling with tears.

She looked fatigued and depressed, "It's true I hated her. I loved Vivek. He always flirted with me. I thought he cared. But apparently after she won the contest, he was only interested in her. He never looked at me again. I began to hate her. "

Sean put in, "So you went to her home with the plan of drugging her and then killing her."

"Yes, I planned it. I went over to her home because I knew she wanted to talk to me about Vivek. I sensed her mistrust. I put three sleeping tablets in her soft drink. I pretended I wanted a drink and went to her kitchen and prepared two drinks. She drank hers and felt woozy. It was easy leading her slowly while she was groggy to the balcony and pushing her out. She was so light, I am at least ten kilos heavier. All that dieting she does made her a lightweight for me. "

She buried her face in her hands, "I thought Vivek would care but he never wanted anything to do with me. I tried to contact him and he told me not to bother him again after two or three calls. He did not want me, I realised. I killed her for nothing. But I hated her. She had everything- looks, fame and would become rich soon with her celebrity status. I knew our friendship was going to break up because she had seen me trying to flirt with Vivek and had suspected I liked him. Lately, she had begun to ignore me. Even at her home on the last visit, I knew she was a bit antagonistic towards me."

"So you took your revenge and killed her."

Aditi was silent.

Unknown to her, this was being recorded.

Then the two officers stood up and told her that she was under arrest. She would stay behind bars.

Aditi sat there like stone. Then she stood up and allowed them to put handcuffs on her.

A constable was summoned who took her away.

Both Sean and Sheena watched her go.

Ch 20

The newspapers had a field day with the story. The news channels played it to the hilt with their breaking news segments showing a beautiful Simran Chawla with a glittering silver crown on her head, smiling for the cameras, waving to the crowds like the queen she was. Her anxiety and bouts of depression were swept away under the carpet. Nobody wanted to focus on her negative points. Aditi was the evil doer here and Simran was the heroine. Simran was glorified even more these days than when she had been crowned. The public always put stars on higher pedestals when they died prematurely.

Then the happy pictures gave way to photos of Aditi Patel which was a strong contrast to the immaculate beauty of Simran. Her long slightly unkempt frizzy hair, her pleasant but simple unadorned face was an antithesis to Simran's immaculate appearance. Aditi dressed casually chic and this lent her a hip appearance but when compared to the striking elegance of Simran, the two were on opposite sides of the beauty scale. The news reporters hinted of the jealousy angle and played up the unrequited love angle too. It was like a soap opera story and the public gleefully lapped it up.

Simran's parents were interviewed and they seemed happy at getting answers and expressed their thanks to the police especially the CBI who had taken over the case. There were few photos displayed of Inspector Sean Fernandez and Inspector Sheena Rai looking professional in their uniforms. They were also featured posing together and their attractiveness made a good photo. The public liked the look of an attractive, intelligent looking team named the Express Squad and this too was played up quite a lot.

Director General Inspector Verma rang them up, offering his admiration for solving the case so quickly within a space of four weeks.

 He also said, "Get your asses back here, pronto. The case is finished, you enjoyed the limelight, now it's back to work."

Sean said, winking at Sheena, "Yes, sir, its back to work again!"

.

Story 2

The Unexpected Murder

Ch 1

June 21st

"Here is to my latest movie. May it be a blockbuster! It is good enough to become one, so say the critics. May their words come true!"

He raised his glass of orange fruit juice and the others followed suit, murmuring their good wishes. He was Karan Desai, one of Bollywood's top producers. He was of medium height and had a hawk like face. He was not unattractive, however, but his face was aged.

The table was a long one, made of Burma teak. It could accommodate on its beautiful suede carved chairs fifteen people but presently there were just five individuals seated close to him.

On his right was the director Pranoy Roy, a tall bearded man with a slightly lean face with silver rimmed glasses that lent his face a rather intellectual appearance. His looks scarcely mattered and he favoured long brown or white kurtas paired with black or blue jeans.

On his left, sat the top camera man, Arun Goyal, a slim, short balding man whose shrewd eyes belied his jovial demeanour that was often hale and hearty. He had worked in practically all of Karan Desai movies.

Next to Pranoy Roy sat the beautiful actress, Aruna Shah, who had starred in his latest movie and she looked every inch a movie star with her fair flawless complexion, her black kohl rimmed eyes that were highly expressive and her pouting full lips expertly outlined with soft pink lip-gloss that lent her a feminine yet sensual appearance.

Besides her, sat her co- star, Arjun Singh who was a clean shaven sardar whose rugged good looks and muscular biceps made him a heartthrob of teenagers everywhere.

Opposite them besides Arun Goyal sat the sister of Karan Desai, a stout, sari clad lady, Sarika Sharma who resided in the next penthouse with her husband who was not present.

All five had their glasses raised in toast of the latest movie just released and wished for its success.

Then all five almost simultaneously raised their glasses to their lips.

It was promising to be an enjoyable evening. The glass chandeliers above them glittered like diamonds shedding soft pink light on their faces.

Suddenly all eyes swirled towards the dominant figure at the head of the table, Karan Desai. He was gasping, the glass in his hand had fell on the table, its contents partly spilling. He was gasping for breath and clutching his throat.

His face looked a mottled grey and his eyes bulged.

He made croaking sounds that sounded terrible.

And then to the horror of those present, he slumped across the table.

"For god's sake!" Pranoy Roy always a very decisive active man, sprang up.

He reached out to the inert gasping man and bent over him.

Sarika shrieked in terror and stood up, "Call the ambulance."

Aruna Shah sat still like a motionless statue, her eyes wide pools of horror.

Arun Goyal fished out his mobile and rang for the ambulance, his fingers slightly shaking.

Arjun Singh stunned now moved back his chair and rushed to the inert man quickly, feeling his pulse.

His face grew solemn after a minute as he shook his head, "He is gone!"

"Do not be crazy, it is not possible!" Sarika looked wild with horror. She was visibly trembling, yet she did not go to the man lying with his head slumped on the table. At that moment, it seemed as if all were so astonished and horrified, they were transfixed, unable to react quickly.

At the kitchen entrance stood the butler, Mahesh Swaminathan, looking horrified and he seemed rooted to the spot.

Arun Goyal had called for the ambulance and five minutes later, its siren could be heard screaming along their street.

All five guests sat or stood motionless, their faces stricken, as though they were in a nightmare and hoped they would soon wake up.

Mahesh Swaminathan moved forward as if to go to his master but Sarika said, "Do not touch him now. The ambulance has been called." She looked defeated for she knew her brother was dead.

Ch 2

Inspector Bose sat at his desk in the Parel police station, looking through the files on his desk.

He went through the autopsy report carefully, his eyes scanning the report as if searching for hidden clues.

The autopsy report was straightforward and concise. It was written by the Medical Examiner, Dr Madhu Srinivas.

She was an eminent forensic pathologist who had assisted the police in various cases with her careful, detailed forensic reports.

According to the report, the victim, Karan Desai, aged, fifty-eight was five feet ten inches tall and weighed a hundred and forty pounds. He was below the average weight for his height.

He seemed in good physical condition for his heart and other organs showed no signs of any underlying medical condition. However, he had died due to cyanide poisoning.

The cyanide used was sodium cyanide (NaCn) which was a white crystalline powder dissolved in the glass of orange fruit juice.

The bitter almond odour of cyanide was detected. The victim gulped it down quickly causing the poison effects to show immediately and fatally.

The victim had consumed almost three fourths of his glass and the amount used was around ten grams which was lethal.

Death was not instant but it took around five minutes or so with the victim gasping and having a seizure. He slumped on the table because he grew very weak and had lost consciousness.

Even if medical aid had been given immediately, there are doubts if he could have survived given his age and the amount of cyanide used. Time of death was estimated to be around nine that night, June 21st.

The autopsy report also spoke about his stomach contents. It was a short list of the foodstuffs he had eaten that morning and afternoon. But the cause of death had been cyanide in the orange fruit juice. Had cyanide been administered in alcohol, death might have probably not occurred because the presence of alcohol limits the uptake of cyanide in the stomach and alcohol neutralises the effect.

Inspector Bose placed down the autopsy report.

Inspector Bose reflected that since the victim never drank alcohol for the past ten years due to health reasons, he had become very conscious of his health and fitness, the fruit juice with cyanide was lethal.

Strange how his own health consciousness had probably killed him. Not everyone would look at it this way but then he was a police officer and his mind travelled in directions that the common man would scarcely think of.

He knew that a month had passed since the murder and they had no real leads.

There were tons of speculations by the press about the underworld who had been instrumental in his death. Veiled references to his links with the underworld don, Asif Mansuri. It was speculated by colleagues that he had irked the don in some way or the other for their friendship had cooled down over the years.

Inspector Bose had his informers. They were people who seemed innocent and average but they performed important services of being the eyes and ears of the police officers. But his informers had no news. They had their connections to Asif Mansuri's gang but there had been no hint of any plan to murder Karan Desai.

He knew he could rely on his informers and suspected there was truth in this. Most likely it was not Asif Mansuri.

So then who?

In all likelihood, it appeared it was one of the five invited for the small dinner party, yet it seemed ludicrous. All five were his friends, or if not friends, at least they had no known enmity towards him.

He had interviewed every one of them but drawn a blank. They had seemed stunned by the death of Karan Desai. All had expressed their shock and sympathy.

The Commissioner, had rung him up a day ago, telling him that it was a high profile case and the ineptitude of the police was being targeted by the internet, public and media. Hints were given about how Asif Mansuri was involved but he had bribed the police.

Inspector Bose had listened and promised to do his best.

But as he sat there thinking about the case, he thought glumly that it was a tough nut to crack.

Ch3

July twenty- third

Director Verma said, "It's time to fly to Mumbai again to solve the latest case that has hit the headlines."

Sean and Sheena were seated in his office.

Sean queried, "I guess you are talking about the Karan Desai case?"

"None other. It is a case that seems baffling. Of course all sorts of theories are floating about that he was killed by the underworld don, Asif Mansuri. But the police in Mumbai are not sure about this."

"Yeah, I read the newspapers and it is a tough case."

Director Verma said, "Yeah and that is why you two will step in."

Sheena queried, "I know Inspector Bose, and we actually studied in the same year."

"Good, then you should have not much trouble collaborating with the police there. I do not need to tell you both the importance of not ruffling feathers and co-operating with the police in South Mumbai. You two know the ropes, I know but sometimes a reminder should not go amiss."

Both nodded.

Director Verma said, "You will fly to Mumbai tomorrow by the ten o'clock flight. You should reach in a few hours and stay at the Andheri guest house. Commuting might be a problem but I prefer that both of you stay at the CBI guest house. I have no idea how long this case will take to solve and have no intention of housing you in some fancy hotel- we got to think of the tax payers you know." He smiled a bit as he said this to take away the sting of his words.

Both nodded agreeably. They liked the guest house and had found it comfortable, commuting was no hardship to them. They had worked in harsher conditions in the past.

Then after a quick briefing, the meeting was concluded.

The next day.

The plane touched down at twelve in the afternoon at Mumbai's Chhatrapati Shivaji Maharaj International airport. It had been a pleasant flight.

They reached the guest house two hours later that afternoon.

Ramesh, the caretaker greeted them with a smile.

They both had the same rooms.

Two of the other rooms at the far corner was occupied by other CBI officers working in a drug case.

Sean said, "We will as usual eat together. Then work on the case, right?"

"Right."

The chemistry lurked between the two but both had no intention at present of pursuing the attraction that lingered like a shadow between them. They were both professionals and knew how to keep their professional distance.

Then they both went into their adjoining rooms and unpacked, then freshened up after the flight.

Ch 4

Three hours later.

The drive to the South Mumbai took more than an hour but it was not unpleasant with the air-conditioner on full blast.

Alok drove them, his silence deferential but he had loosened up a bit and told them that his son had been hospitalised for appendicitis and was now better. They listened and put in a sympathetic word that cheered him up.

Inspector Bose greeted them quite affably. He recognized Sheena instantly and they both chatted about the past for a few minutes. He was the kind of man who was friendly and reminded Sheena of a big teddy bear. But she did know that his friendly looks belied his intelligence for he had a good track record of solving cases.

He filled them up with all the details of the ongoing investigation. After this, he settled back in his chair and said, "Here is the file with all the relevant information. As I told you, we interviewed all the guests at the dinner party but have drawn a blank because they all seem above suspicion. Yet obviously one of them is most likely the killer."

Sean said, "We will work together on this and I will keep you updated."

"Yeah, sure. You know I am pleased you guys are taking over. I have right now on my hands an important case of the murder of a prostitute. It will never get headlines but I am determined to nab the killer. Just because a lady is a sex worker, it does not mean she is inhuman and her life is worthless. Got a few leads and hope to crack the case soon." He looked fairly optimistic and they were sure, he had a good idea about who the killer was.

Then, after a cup of piping hot tea, Sean and Sheena left.

Sean decided to begin the interviews with the dinner guests that evening.

He did not want to waste time. They had live up to the reputation of being called the Express Squad and it was not easy. In fact, it could be daunting but this never fazed him unduly. He knew most cases were like jigsaw puzzles. They seemed difficult and made at times little sense. Yet, once many of the pieces were joined together, a pattern began to appear and there was light at the end of the tunnel.

The duty of theirs was to join the pieces together and though it seemed hard, it was never impossible. Every case however, difficult could be solved especially if evidence was stored carefully and no stone left unturned.

Ch 5

That evening, Sean and Sheena sat opposite Arjun Singh in his makeup van in the film studio.

He was quite eager to assist in any way possible.

One got the impression that Arjun Singh was an affable kind of guy, not arrogant or overbearing in the least. His rugged handsome looks and friendly smile were quite magnetic and Sheena who had worked on cases involving celebrities still found herself getting impressed. No wonder the man was set to become one the biggest names in Bollywood.

His makeup artist left the van after Arjun told him he needed to talk to them privately.

The lights of the big mirror cast his face in soft incandescent light, and his makeup was applied expertly. Sheena knew in all likelihood he never needed makeup but under the harsh glare of lights, he could look washed out and hence he wore the requisite makeup. Arjun sat quite comfortably in his vanity chair that was upholstered in red suede.

It was decided by them prior to this meeting that Sean would conduct the interview and in the last five minutes, Sheena would take over.

Sean began, keeping the recorder on. Arjun was informed that the interview would be recorded and seemed to have no objections.

He simply said, "Shoot, man!"

Sean began, "First, tell us how well you know the deceased Karan Desai?"

Arjun said easily, "I knew him for a number of years. I began my career five years ago and he had been a friend of the family. It was he who gave me my first break in the movie, *Insaaf.*"

He paused, then said, "It was not a blockbuster but did fairly well at the box office. But Karan Desai never gave up on me. We worked together in another movie, *Dhan*, and this was a massive hit. I became an overnight household name. Lately, we had just completed this new movie, *Sitara* that he was hoping would be a blockbuster."

Sean asked, "What were the guests including yourself drinking?"

Arjun said, "I think we all drank champagne but only Karan drank fruit juice. I think it was an orange fruit juice. He was very health conscious."

Sean said, "Tell me the position of each of you on the table."

"Yeah, well, at his right sat Pranoy Roy, then Aruna Shah and I sat beside her. On his left sat Arun Goyal and Karan's sister, Sarika Sharma."

"Who served the drinks?"

"The drinks were served by a butler, the guy had been with Karan for the past ten years. Karan always wanted to have a proper butler, it kind of tickled his fancy. His name is Mahesh Swaminathan, a south Indian from Madras. But I think he was okay, quite deferential and quiet."

"Did any of you leave the table?"

Arjun said, "Yes, funny enough, after the drinks were served, Karan had told us to come into his private room that housed his art objects. He had a room that housed his art collection. I mean the stuff was not Picasso or anything. It was just good stuff that he had bought from art galleries. He often patronised paintings by upcoming painters, for he told us that many could become the next Hussain and besides he liked art. I think he liked art from his childhood and even showed us a few paintings in his living room that he had painted. You know the typical Indian rural scenes featuring women exposing their mid-riffs and tight sari type blouses. He was pretty good, I have to say."

"So how long did you spend in his private art room?"

'Well, about fifteen minutes and I remember, Karan had carried his glass of fruit juice with him and sipped it. But as he was talking about one of the modern art paintings, he set it down on the side-table."

"I see. So basically any of you could have spiked the drink." Sean said reflectively.

"Yeah, that is true. Inspector Bose too said the same thing. But why would we do that? We all liked him."

Sean did not comment.

Then it was Sheena's turn. "Did Karan have any known enemies?"

Arjun shrugged, "Look, when you are as successful as this guy, you are bound to cross a few people. But offhand, I could not say, honestly."

Sheena asked, "Given a choice of all the dinner guests, if you could pick one, who would you choose?"

Arjun raised his eyebrows, "Ah! Tough question but honestly none of us. Unless you think his sister, Sarika had something to do with it. I heard that he had left most of his money to her being a bachelor. So, that could be a possibility. Human greed is deadly."

After this, there was a knock on his van door and the spot boy was outside telling him that shooting had to commence.

Sean stood up with Sheena and said, "If we have further queries, we will let you know."

Arjun smiled, "Sure, anytime. I liked Karan Desai and I hope his killer will be caught."

Sean and Sheena left the film studio.

Alok drove them to the next place as ordered by Sean which was Sarika Sharma's residence.

Ch 6

Sarika Sharma resided in the same building as the deceased, Karan Desai. In fact, their penthouses were on the same floor, opposite each other. Sean knew Karan's home was locked but he had the key to go in if he wanted to. He would go in after talking to Sarika Sharma. Karan's maid servant and butler were now residing in Sarika's home.

The cream building looked fairly new and had the look of upper middle class. The flat was situated on the fifteenth floor.

The ornate white door was opened by a tall well-built man dressed in black trousers and a cream shirt.

Sean guessed that he was the butler, Mahesh Swaminathan. He looked a bit unhappy, and his face looked drawn.

Sean introduced themselves and the Mahesh said, "Please come in. Madam is at home."

He led the way down a long passage that opened to a big spacious living room with marble flooring. It was well decorated but did not have an interior designer's stamp on it. It looked as if Sarika had decorated it herself and it had a homely pleasant vibe to it.

They sat on the comfortable black and red sofas and waited. It had been decided that Sheena would first begin the interview and then Sean would take over.

Sarika Sharma entered, looking a bit hassled.

"Sorry to keep you waiting but I was on my computer."

She had a stern expression on her face but when she smiled, one got the distinct impression that she had a kind heart.

She sat down heavily opposite them on the long black divan and though she was not obese, she was plump and matronly. Yet, she gave off a homely vibe that was quite surprising. Both had expected a hard faced socialite type, who looked expensive and obsessive about money.

Sarika said, "Please have something to drink. It is a hot day, isn't it?"

As if on cue, Mahesh appeared and she told him to bring her guests some soft drinks.

Mahesh inclined his head and walked away. He walked quite ramrod straight and it was clear that he was a well -trained butler.

Sarika leant forward and whispered conspiratorially, "He really is a dear. So well trained and hardworking. I understand now why Karan was so fond of him. After, my brother's ……" Her voice trembled slightly, "Well, after his death, Mahesh wanted to go back to his native village in Chennai but I forbade him. Even the maid wanted to leave but I asked her to stay on. She works part-time at my home and the neighbours down below. The maid, Paru, is a very quiet lady who is hardworking and so far honest. I kept both of them on. You know Mahesh belongs to an upper caste, but he was not educated enough for his parents died in his youth."

"I see." Sheena said, "Now, I hope you do not mind us asking you a few questions. I know it is a hard time but do bear with us."

This approach seemed to work well for Sarika brightened up.

Just then, Mahesh walked in with a tray bearing two tall glasses of watermelon juice that looked freshly squeezed and a plate of potato chips.

Sarika urged them to first have the juice and snacks and then begin the questions.

They agreed. She had a kind of maternal air that made them feel as if they were in the presence of some elderly well- meaning aunty.

Then when they had enjoyed the juice and snacks, Sheena assumed a professional air.

Her tone was brisk but pleasant as she questioned, "Were you really very surprised when your brother was poisoned? Think carefully because your answer is important to us. Maybe you were not that surprised, he may have had enemies."

They both waited as she pondered on the question.

She seemed intelligent and she took her time answering. She finally said, "No, I cannot say. I understand that as he was so successful, he may have had enemies but I really did not interfere much in the life of my brother, Karan, personal or professional. You know I tried to get him married. I had arranged for him to see a few girls around ten years ago but he refused all of them. They had been pretty, nice young women but he was never interested in marriage. I realised that he was a confirmed bachelor and then gave up trying to see him settled. I know that the rumours abound that all I wanted was his money but I really wanted him to marry and it had been his choice to remain a bachelor. In his will he left his money to me. He left a small amount of Rupees five lakhs each for his servants- Mahesh and the maid, Paru. I have three kids, all in America, either working or studying. I am older than Karan by ten years, in my sixties. I never coveted his money, not like the rumours floating about. I read the gossip columns you know, I know what they say. Of course everyone likes money and I am happy to get it, it will be mostly for my kids. My husband Rakesh is a business man and doing well. But I was never devious to try to plot to get the cash for myself. It had been his choice not to marry and to leave his money to me. Our parents died ten years ago. We were the only children."

After this, tears began in her eyes and she sniffed.

Her grief seemed genuine. It was hard to believe she could have poisoned her brother. Yet both were well versed with murderers who possessed great acting ability and could convince even a cynic they innocent.

So the important part of being professional was to keep an open mind. Sean knew the dictum- Guilty till proved innocent. It was the maxim he took.

Sheena said gently, "I understand this is hard for you but please bear with us."

Sarika looked at her, feeling a bit better for Sheena despite her brisk air could be very gentle when she chose to.

Sheena said, "Is it true that Karan took you all to his room where he displayed his paintings?"

Sarika nodded, "Yes, Mahesh had served our drinks and Karan was sipping from his. Suddenly he decided on a whim to show us his paintings. He stood up with his glass and took it to the art room with him. I remember him showing us this painting of a beautiful lady, standing next to a waterfall, scantily clothed. All the guys made ribald jokes. He placed his glass down on the side-table. We all gazed at the painting for it looked very realistic and the model was stunningly lovely. I think the guys could not tear their eyes off from the model who had this......" She blushed faintly, "This come hither look in her eyes. I felt a bit embarrassed and moved to look at another painting."

"I see, what about Aruna Shah?"

Sarika said vaguely, "Come to think of it, I could not say. I cannot remember, she must have been with the guys. I was not close to her, in the sense I did not really know her. I thought I saw her standing alone gazing at a painting but I paid little attention. In fact I hardly ever spoke to her. I just knew she was acting in Karan's newly released movie."

Sean took over now.

He asked, "Can we talk to Mahesh Swaminathan, please."

Sarika said quickly, "Yes, of course."

She went into the servant's quarters and two minutes later emerged with Mahesh Swaminathan.

Ch 7

Mahesh Swaminathan looked cool and calm, his butler manner not betraying his emotions. But there were dark shadows around his eyes that spoke of tiredness due to anxiety.

Sarika sat down and Mahesh remained standing, with a dignified yet deferential air.

Sean said, "I want you to tell me in your own words everything that you remember on that fatal night at the dinner party. Do not be afraid to get into detail. Just imagined the scene in front of you and tell me everything."

Mahesh seemed intelligent for he nodded, "Yes, sir. I will do my best."

He was silent for a minute and then he said, "The guests arrived at around eight or so. Some a little later, but all came before eight-thirty. They knew my master, was a stickler for punctuality."

He darted a swift look at Sarika, who nodded encouragingly.

Then he went on, "I was at the kitchen with Paru who was cooking the dinner for the guests. I remember that she had prepared a pulao, chicken curry, potato patties, and paneer butter masala and had prepared two salads. For dessert she had made a chocolate mousse. We were chatting in the kitchen because we got along well. Then it was time to serve the drinks. I went into the dining room and placed glasses on the table. I served my master orange fruit juice. The others were served champagne which I poured into their glasses. Then I left and was in the kitchen helping Paru to put the snacks on the trays. I heard my master telling the guests to come and see the new paintings in his room. I understood then not to serve the snacks. I peered out and saw all their glasses on the table except my master's glass. I realised that he had taken it with him. And then I heard them coming back perhaps twenty minutes later or so. The kitchen door is connected to the dining room so I could see and hear everything. They were chatting loudly. I did not enter again but waited till they finished their drinks."

Sean asked, "So tell me, what did you see or hear just before he died."

 Mahesh said solemnly, "Actually, I heard him talk about his new movie and I guessed they were raising their glasses like a toast. At the moment, I was helping Paru to check where she had kept the strawberries for decoration to top the mousse. I rummaged through the fridge and found the strawberries hidden behind the packets of frozen vegetables. And I heard a scream and lots of people getting upset. I handed her the strawberries and went into the dining room."

He paused and he looked a bit distraught, "My master was slumped across the table. He was dead. I wanted to rush and touch him but Arjun Singh was taking his pulse and the others were surrounding his body. I thought it was a heart attack. So I remained where I was standing at the kitchen door. I wanted to go to him but madam….' He gestured to Sarika continuing, "Told me to wait for the ambulance."

He looked more distraught now and although he tried to keep a cool butler demeanour, it was clear that he was very upset.

Sarika said, "I guess that will be all, Mahesh."

She knew that he needed time to compose himself.

Sean nodded as Mahesh walked ramrod straight back to his room. He had his own bedroom just adjacent to the kitchen.

Sean said, "We would like to speak to Paru."

Sarika frowned, "Well, she ought to be here but today she is late."

As if on cue, the doorbell rang. It was Paru.

She was an elderly looking lady, in actual fact she was only in her fifties but she looked twenty years older. She wore a blue faded cotton sari, her thin hair in a small bun, her weathered dusky face pleasant.

Sarika explained the police officers wanted to talk to her. For a moment she looked alarmed but Sarika said reassuringly, "Just few minutes, Paru."

 Paru nodded.

Sean asked, "It was you who prepared the food that day for the party?"

"Yes, sir."

Paru looked nervous.

Sean asked, "What about fruit juice?" Paru looked a bit alarmed. She darted a swift nervous look at Sarika but Sarika nodded encouragingly.

She said nervously, "Yes, sir. I poured the orange fruit juice from the fruit juice carton. The police took away the carton with them. That is all I did. I did not do anything, sir. Mahesh, then took the fruit juice in the glass to the master. I did not poison him. The police got the carton with them. "

Sean looked at her a bit sternly, "But you could have put something in the juice?"

Paru drew herself up proudly. There was a look of pride on her face now. "Sir, I would never poison my master. He was so good to me. I wanted to work for him."

"Did you know about the will? He had left you five lakhs."

Paru nodded, "Yes, five lakhs. It is a lot of money for me. He had opened a bank account for me and under the stipulation of the will the money would go into my account. He had told me that one day he would provide for me but he never said more. I never questioned him. I just thought that he meant he might give me little financial aid when I grew old. You see, I had every intention of serving him till I could no longer work. The job was good, the pay was better than I expected. In fact after I began working for him, I was more like a whole day maid except at night I used to go home. So I never took on other jobs except if a friend of mine asked me to work in one job as a substitute if she was ill. Then I took permission from my master to do so. I was loyal, sir. I liked my master. I never knew that he would leave me so much money. This money will be used for my old age. I am a widow and my only son is in Dubai working as an electrical engineer for a big company. He sends me money, enough to live decently. But what can I do alone at home? So I worked and any money is always good for us poor people. I save as much as I can. "

She seemed sincere and both of them found her believable.

But still Sean had to keep an open mind.

He knew no poison had been placed in the carton of juice except in the glass.

He knew nothing more could be got from her so he said, "Okay, you may go but if we want to question you, you will be summoned by us."

Paru nodded and walked into the kitchen, looking a bit more relieved. Like all lower classes, she had a dread of the police. She believed the police would always take the side of the rich, not the poor. It was a belief that was hard to shake off.

Sarika sighed, "I wish you could find whoever did this. I want justice too, yet even if I get justice, nothing will bring back Karan. So justice is something like revenge, it can be a double- edged sword."

After this, Sean and Sheena took their leave.

Ch 8

Sean and Sarika visited Karan's home. It was a beautiful home. They walked around. They went into the art room. They saw beautiful paintings displayed on the walls. There was the painting of the beautiful woman, scantily clad by the waterfall that had attracted the males. They stood by it and Sheena murmured, "It is an arresting painting admittedly."

Sean spotted the side-table at a corner on which Karan had placed his glass of orange juice.

They spent an hour in the flat but found nothing of real interest that could help them in the case. They decided to then leave.

On their way back to the guest house, Sean asked Sheena, "So what do you think?"

Sheena looked up from her mobile and said, "What do I think? I think everybody is guilty right now, we cannot eliminate any suspect. Guilty till proven innocent. Someone had a motive and we got to find out that motive. Money, love, revenge, those are the angles that lead to murder. We have to find out which motive was strong enough for someone to murder him. It has to be one of these three."

"Money wise, it could be Sarika, Paru or Mahesh."

"Yes, now what about love?"

"Love? He is rumoured not to be involved with anyone. A confirmed bachelor."

"What about Aruna Shah? Could he have been involved with her?"

"Well, we have to explore that angle." Sean said reflectively. "She is next on my list for an interview."

"Okay, now revenge. It is rumoured that Asif Mansuri might have plotted to kill him but all the informants have no knowledge of this and that is impossible given the fact our police informants are good at what they do. So if the revenge angle is to be considered then again we have to consider each one of our suspects. So revenge wise it does not narrow it down, it just makes you realise we cannot eliminate anyone." Sean surmised.

Sheena always offered some light even if the long tunnel ahead was pitch black. She had an uncanny way of hitting on pertinent points. He knew without her, he would lag behind in spite of his cleverness and instinct for detection. She was like his right hand partner and he always considered her his equal. In this relationship, it was not a case of- "I am Sherlock and you are Watson." She was his equal partner, both in brains and police detection. He never underestimated her.

They reached the guest house and had their lunch.

Then both spent the afternoon compiling their report. Then they sent it to Director Verma by e mail.

Ch 9

That evening, both set off to meet actress Aruna Shah.

Her manager had picked up her mobile because she had been shooting at that time. He confirmed after ten minutes that Aruna would see them in her flat at nine that night after shooting.

They promised to be there. It was no use compelling film stars to comply like normal people at least during the initial stages. So they both had to go along with the flow. They knew her residential address from Inspector Bose's file on the case.

They both had their dinner followed by a light dessert of a fruit salad. Then, they set off with Alok who drove them to the tall peach and cream building complex that looked impressive. The compound boasted of a large rectangular swimming pool in the right corner. The waters looked pristine blue.

The security guard let them in without a murmur. Aruna Shah resided in building no 5.

The high speed lift took them to the sixth floor of the tenth floor high rise. The complex had six buildings that were similar in appearance. The complex had big grounds that were cemented and a separate area for kids that had well shorn grass and even an area for adults to exercise on the various exercise equipment provided. It was obviously for affluent people.

The flat number was 601 and there was on her teak polished door a large black nameplate with gold lettering with her name. There were three flats per floor. There were potted plants placed strategically around on the red carpeted floor.

On ringing the doorbell, a maid opened the door. She was elderly and had a sharp expression on her weather beaten face.

They introduced themselves and she permitted them to step in.

She led them through a long passage decorated with a few carved mirrors and photos of Aruna Shah posing happily. The maid told them to be seated and that madam would see them.

Minutes later, Aruna Shah entered the big opulent living room, looking every inch a star. She had not yet made it to the biggest league in Bollywood but she certainly was climbing up the ladder of stardom.

Sean saw a beautiful poised lady whose inscrutable face revealed little. Sheena felt quite drab in comparison in blue jeans and a red cropped top.

Aruna, clad in a silk green kurta and black fitting pants with a chiffon white and green dupatta looked very chic and poised. Her makeup was immaculate for she had just returned from shooting.

Her face though looked fresh and vibrant and there was no visible signs of fatigue. She seemed calm and very poised. Her figure was slim and she was a few pounds underweight for her height of five feet eight inches. Yet, this was perfect for clothes to fall well on her slim frame.

She crossed her legs gracefully and sat straight.

Sheena found herself unconsciously straightening her posture. Odd she reflected how poised beautiful women made one feel inadequate so quickly.

Aruna looked at Sean and in her glance there was an aware look that leapt up. It was a womanly look and it had a subtle flirtatious quality to it.

Sean however, ignored that look and schooled his face to be bland.

Aruna raised her well- shaped and pencilled eyebrows. "I guess this is about the Karan Desai case?" she drawled.

Sheena said shortly, "You guessed right. The interview will be recorded."

Aruna nodded.

Sheena said," I want you to tell us in your own words about that evening."

There was a pause and Aruna said, "Okay, let's see. I went for the dinner at around eight-fifteen, I mean I reached there at that time. I know because I glanced at my watch and saw the time. Karan liked punctuality, he hated tardiness. Well, we all said hello to him and to each other. I had never met his sister, Sarika Sharma and I was introduced to her. She said hello but we did not chat. I think she was kind of reserved, the type who did not gush over anyone."

She paused and then went on in her well-modulated voice, "Well, the butler, his name is Mahesh I think came with the tray of glasses. Karan was served his fruit juice, orange fruit juice, while, our empty glasses were put on the table. Then Mahesh poured champagne from the bottle as Karan instructed him to. We were chatting casually. Karan did not sip his drink. He suddenly announced he wanted to show us his paintings. He took his glass with him. We all went to the room and were admiring his collection. I think he did place his glass down on the side-table and was enthusiastic about talking about his art collection, particularly a new one featuring a beautiful young woman near a waterfall. All the guys were gaga over it. Sarika felt a bit embarrassed and she moved away."

"What about you?" Sheena questioned.

Aruna said, "Well, I moved away to look at another painting. It was of a scenery, a mountain and some lake."

"Was this painting next to the side-table where Karan placed his glass?' Sheena asked coolly.

Aruna said, "As a matter of fact, it was. Sarika too, was adjacent to me, looking at another painting of a vase with roses. We both moved away, looking at the other paintings. In the meanwhile, Karan was asking us to look at a painting of a tiger and we did so. Then we all left. He took his glass with him. At the table, he proposed a toast for the success of his film, he raised his glass to his lips and then…….."

She paused, "He grew quite red and was gasping. We thought that he was having a stroke or a heart attack. Then he slumped across the table his breathing laboured. The guys sprang into action and Arjun took his pulse. Then Arjun told us he had passed away. We thought it was a heart attack but we were horrified. It was so totally unexpected."

She paused and looked less calm now, "Arun Goyal called the ambulance. They came quite quickly. The doctor there told us he was dead after a brief examination. They took his body away. They told Sarika to come to the hospital later. We all were shocked. Sarika began to cry. The guys did not know what to do. But Mahesh came to us and told us to leave and we listened to him. I mean he really can act liked an English butler when he wants. So that is it."

There was a bit of silence after this as Aruna seemed a bit tearful. She sniffed and looked like she was about to cry.

Sean asked, "Did you see anyone tampering with the glass of Karan's?"

Aruna shook her head, "No, no one. We were all admiring the paintings, so we did not really notice each other's actions. You know how it is. When people look at interesting things, they rarely notice what their neighbour is doing."

"A perfect opportunity for the killer." Sean said grimly.

Aruna agreed, "I guess so."

"Tell me Aruna, did you know Karan well?"

"Well, I had acted in his newly released movie. I did not know him really well. He was an okay guy."

"So you never knew him before personally except professionally?" Sheena asked.

Aruna looked at her coolly and shook her head, "No, just professionally. "

Sean took over, "Perhaps you have some theory as to why and who could have poisoned him. We would be happy at your inputs."

Aruna thought for a while but she shook her head, "I cannot say. I know the newspapers talk about Asif Mansuri but who knows? It could be him. I know from the reports, Karan had broken off a lot of contact with him. He had financed some of Karan's movies as a partner. But Karan was looking for other partners, I guess the other underworld dons who had approached him."

Sen looked at her cool face and thought she really was a cool customer. The kind that did not get rattled easily. Her beauty was sensuously mesmerising and it was little wonder that she was on a sure path to stardom in the big league.

He knew there would be little to get from her for she was beginning to look a bit fed up as if the interview bored her.

Sean said, "Alright, that's all for now. If we do have any questions, we will contact you."

Aruna said, "Do that but talk to my manager, he arranges everything."

"Sure." He decided to play the game her way. Celebrities were best dealt with carefully. He hardly wanted to upset her unduly because he knew the policy of Director Verma was that while dealing with public figures, it was imperative to use diplomacy.

They took their leave.

On the way home, Sean looked at Sheena, "Well?"

Sheena shrugged, "A cool customer, not easily rattled. But you know what? When I asked her if she knew Karan personally, I fancy a kind of wary look crept into those lovely eyes of hers. I think the lady is not being truthful. I think we ought to delve into her past a bit more."

Sean thought about this, "You are right. We will do a little sleuthing about our beautiful actress's past."

They made their way back to the guest house.

Ch 10

It was decided that Sheena would delve into Aruna Shah's past. It would be a bit time consuming but she knew she could do it.

Sean then decided to tackle the next suspect- Pranoy Roy, the director of his last movie.

Pranoy Roy was contacted and he told them to visit his home at seven that evening.

They knew his residential address from the police files. Alok drove them along the streets that were quieter and the lanes narrower as they neared Chembur where he resided.

Then, he halted next to a small cottage that looked newly painted. The garden was small but well kept, though there were several weeds growing haphazardly. Tall trees lined the edges. An old security guard sat outside on an old chair. He was chewing paan and looked at them with mild interest as Sean and Sheena walked towards the front gate.

Sean said, "Mr Roy is expecting us."

The security guard nodded and reached for the intercom on the wall next to him. He spoke briefly and then told them, "Go in. Mr Roy is expecting you."

They walked in, through the long cemented pathway that led to entrance. There was a small flight of steps at a corner rather than at the middle. It led directly to a long veranda with a table and chairs.

They heard footsteps. A tall intellectual looking man with silver spectacles emerged and greeted then affably.

He had a charming manner and he seemed the type who would get along with most people. After Sean had introduced himself and Sheena, Pranoy Roy bade them to be seated.

They all sat on the red plastic chairs around the red plastic table in the veranda. It was not hot for there was plenty of breeze around that helped dispel the morning's heat.

Pranoy Roy seemed quite at ease and one got the distinct impression that little would worry this man. His cool, inscrutable face revealed little of his emotions. He had the kind of bland poker face that was hard to read. No would never really guess his private thoughts. Despite his affable manner, he seemed a closed book. These were the first impressions both got from him.

Sean said, "We will be recording this interview."

"No objections." Pranoy said easily, "Just shoot."

It had been decided that Sean would take over the initial questioning. So he asked, "Please recount the events of that day when Karan died." Pranoy Roy agreed. He said that he reached the home of Karan Desai at eight-thirty. His story was the same account that the rest had told. However, the only difference was that he said nobody could have poisoned Karan because all of them were looking at the paintings in the art room. He could not recall anyone hampering with the glass of orange juice.

Sean said, "But it could be that one of the people present stole away from the group and put the poison in the glass. It would not take more than a few seconds."

Pranoy had to agree. But he pointed out, "We were all involved in the movie except Sarika the sister. We had nothing to gain by killing him. The only person who had anything to gain and by that I mean monetary gain from him was Sarika Sharma."

It was clear that Pranoy Roy suspected the sister as the top suspect.

Sean said, "Perhaps but we need more evidence before we can accuse anyone."

"This murder might remain one of those unsolved crimes you read about. What are they called? Ah, yes, cold cases."

Sheena said a bit coldly, "Perhaps, but we are doing our best to solve it and to see it does not fall into the cold case category."

Pranoy had a slight smile on his face. He shrugged, "Yeah, all the best!"

Sheena raised her eyebrows a bit. She guessed he was one of those smart guys who liked to have the last word.

She asked, "What kind of relationship did you share with Karan?"

Pranoy said quickly, "We got along pretty well."

Sheena pointed out, "But some unit members said that you two had differences on the set when Karan came to visit the film studio." She knew this from the interviews with some crew members by Inspector Bose who had put this on the police case file.

"Look, these things always happen. He was the producer putting in the capital and I was director doing my best to make the movie a success. Of course some clashes might occur. He wanted a wet sari scene in the movie where Aruna Shah danced in the rain seductively. I told him it was too common and Sridevi and others had done it. We should try to be original. I suggested a scene in which she dresses in western clothes to seduce the hero Arjun Singh. But he was very insistent about the white wet sari scene. In the end we compromised and we used a soft pink sari and though far from original, it was okay enough I guess. The critics seemed to like it. That only shows there is never a sure fire formula for taste."

He had a wry smile on his face.

He was not handsome in the strictest conventional sense but he was definitely attractive.

Sean asked, "Did Karan hint of any problem that he was facing? Either personal or professional?"

Pranoy thought for a moment, then shook his head, "No, he and I shared a professional relationship. If you knew Karan you would realise that he was a reserved person, not much into exchanging confidences. So I had no idea about any personal problems."

"What about on the professional front?" Sheena queried.

Pranoy said, "I cannot be sure about anything but there were rumours."

"What rumours? Sheena asked.

'Well, he was going to tie up with another underworld don, most likely, Ahmed Ali. Ali would finance his next movie not Asif Mansuri. I have no idea why but I heard this. Personally, Karan never breathed a word to me. He was a bit secretive like that. You see if you knew him well, you would realise that he was very reserved and had quite a poker look on his face. One never really knew what he was thinking." He saw Sheena's expression and he laughed, "Yeah, I know I too got a bit of a poker face, have been told about it once or twice, but Karan was in a league of his own. No telling the thoughts that went through his head. Not speaking ill of him, just telling you facts."

Then, Pranoy's mobile began to ring. It was a unit member.

He spoke for two minutes and then cut the call.

"Shooting is scheduled tomorrow and the set has to be ready, so have the extras. But one of the main extras is ill so we got to find another. Problems never cease, do they?" He said wryly.

Both of them realised that there was nothing more to be learnt.

Sean said, "We will contact you if we need to talk again."

"Sure." Pranoy said easily.

They walked to the car, and Alok drove them back to the guesthouse in Andheri.

Ch 11

The next on their list was Arun Goyal, a slim, short man who was balding. He had a jovial manner but his eyes were cynical and knowing.

They met him at the film studio. Shooting had just got over.

The stars had retired back to their vanity vans.

Arun was with his crew and he called out, "Will be with you in a minute."

His minute took close to half an hour but both Sean and Sheena patiently waited.

Then, he came to meet them at the lobby of the film studio with an apologetic look on his face, "Sorry about that, but I came as fast as I could."

Sean nodded and gestured him to be seated on the chairs that the security guard after learning that they were police officers, brought for them.

Arun sat down and he looked at both inquiringly.

His face had a slight tenseness about it that perhaps was normal for few people really looked relaxed talking to police officers or being questioned as suspects by them.

"So am I a suspect? Is this what it is about?" Arun asked, looking a bit anxious. It was clear that the thought upset him.

Sean reassured him, "Listen, we have to find answers and all of you were present there so we need to get your input."

This approach seemed to work. Arun visibly relaxed.

He said gamely, "Go ahead, shoot! I will co-operate to my best ability."

His eyes were intent on Sean.

He was a typical man chauvinist who would prefer a male, Sean, doing the questioning.

Sean read out his statement given to Inspector Bose. He had recounted that evening and it was similar to all the accounts the other had given. There was nothing new.

Arun listened and nodded, "Correct. This is what happened."

Sean said, "Is there anything you would like to add? When time passes, one remembers things that might not seem important but could be pertinent in the case. So take your time."

Arun thought for a long moment.

He then said slowly, "I think either Mahesh the butler or Sarika, his sister did it. It makes sense. Mahesh served the drink to him and if not him, then Sarika spiked his drink somehow. She got a lot you know, from his will. Clever lady."

Sean said, "Yes, but it was Paru also who poured out the fruit juice."

"So maybe Mahesh and Paru are in league together. I mean they both benefited by his will."

"Yes, perhaps .Both work now for his sister, Sarika." Sean pointed out, "They hardly grabbed the money and ran."

Arun lowered his voice, "I think all three could be in it together. That would explain a lot."

Sean said wryly, "Unfortunately, this is not a Bollywood movie, but real life. So we need facts before we accuse anyone, let alone put them behind bars."

"True." Arun fell silent, suspecting his insights to the case were not as fantastic as he imagined.

Sheena asked, "Did Karan have any enemies?"

Arun said slowly, "Well, in this movie business one can ruffle feathers you know. It's a million buck industry. But I really do not know much. Heard he was trying to tie in with Ahmed Ali the don, but it could be rumours. He never said so to me anyway. Kind of a private kind of guy. Hard to read really but I liked working in his movies. He was an okay guy in many ways. He paid well enough and I remember when my wife was ill, he sent her flowers in the hospital. I have one kid, he is in school, just ten years old. Karan once sent him a birthday present on his fourth birthday. It was a helicopter, a remote battery operated one because Akash, my son wanted one. I had told this in passing to Karan and a week later on my son's birthday, he sent the helicopter. My son was overjoyed. So yes, I think he had a good heart. But I never knew much about his personal life. I do not think that he was a womaniser. Of course, he had dated girls in the past but these days he was more work oriented. I think he thought age was catching up with him. It's catching up with all of us." He touched his balding head wryly.

There was a bit of a silence after this.

Sheena noticed Arun looked a bit sad as if he regretted the death of Karan Desai.

He said glumly, "Karan has been missed."

Sean then asked, "Did you see anything suspicious that day."

"What do you mean by suspicious?" Arun raised his eyebrows.

Sean clarified, "By suspicious I mean whether you recall anything on that night that might shed more light on the murder of Karan Desai. After all, you seem like an observant and intelligent man, so you may recall something pertinent."

This had the desired effect. Arun thought for a while, looking considerably more cheerful and said, "I remember when we were staring at that painting of the beautiful damsel near the waterfall, Arjun said that she looked like a Bollywood star. Aruna Shah made a face and retorted that men always judged women on their physical appearance. Then Aruna and Sarika left the group and were wandering about looking at the other paintings. I remember thinking that women were so sensitive about certain things and get upset so easily. Well, I cannot recall anything else of interest."

Sean nodded, "Thank you for your time. If we need to contact you, we will ring you up."

Arun Goyal stood up, "Yes, of course. Glad to help."

Then both Sean and Sheena left, joining Alok in the car that took them to the South Mumbai police station at Parel. On his mobile a message flashed that Inspector Bose wanted to talk to them.

Ch 12

At the police station, Inspector Bose told them the latest news from their informers.

Apparently, Asif Mansuri was not involved in Karan's death because at the time of his murder Asif was in Dubai. Besides his trusted henchmen who performed any nefarious activities like murder had accompanied him. Also the informers were positive that Asif Mansuri had not been responsible for the murder of Karan for they had a lot of inside information.

Sean said, "Well, that is good in a way because we can concentrate on the dinner party members and the servants. All those guests have good social status except for the butler and the maid who could be involved."

"Yeah, this sure narrows it down to the suspects- seven in total right? You guys have some sleuthing to do." Inspector Bose said, with a chuckle.

Sean made a face, "Yes that is right. But it sure makes things easier than if we were hunting some unknown serial killer."

Sheena piped in, "Dealt with a serial killer a few years ago. It was a harrowing experience. Give me known suspects anyway!"

"Yeah, but sometimes it gets hard to prove with these filmy types." Sean pointed out.

Inspector Bose agreed.

It was time to leave after a hot cup of coffee.

They left in the car for the guest house, each one wrapped in their own thoughts.

Ch 13

That evening after dinner, Sheena received an e mail.

It was from her uncle who told her that her aunt had expired from a sudden heart attack in Bangalore.

Sheena was shocked and showed the message to a concerned Sean who saw her pale face.

Sheena said, "When my mother died, my aunt was very kind to me. I did not reside with her but she always phoned me up and was such a comforting presence in my life."

Sean said quietly, "Well, I guess you must want to go to Bangalore."

Sheena said, "You know when we are working on a case unless imperative or very urgent, we cannot just take off anywhere."

Sean said quietly, "True."

Then to his immense surprise, Sheena began to cry.

She did not sob hysterically but just sat still, covering her face almost like a child who is afraid of being seen as wimpy.

He let her cry.

Her sobs were soft and a bit muffled but he could see the deep pain behind the tears that fell but were more poignant than had they been loud hysterical crying.

He knew her reserve, her stoic calmness that she prided herself on.

Then, she raised her tear stained face and looked at him, "Sorry about that."

"Nothing to be sorry about. It's natural. She was like a kind of mother figure to you. I would feel like sobbing too."

Sheena made a face, "Not you!"

Sean said quietly, "You would be surprised. "

There was a short silence between them. Then Sean said, "Your divorce, your husband's death, now this, we are all human you know, things take their emotional toll on the most strongest of us."

Sheena shrugged, "Yes."

She wiped her tears, sniffing but strove to maintain her composure.

Then she rang up her uncle and spoke to him.

Sean left the room to give her some privacy.

Then as he sat in the bedroom, flicking through his mobile's messages.

 Sheena called him, "Come out now. "

Sean entered noticing she looked measurably better.

Then both discussed the case.

Sheena said, "Remember we needed to find out more about the background of Aruna Shah. I will work on it tonight."

"Yeah, do that, it might amount to nothing but every angle has to be explored by us. We have to complete the jigsaw puzzle although the pieces right now are hazy. And make little sense."

Sheena then left, leaving Sean to complete his report to Director Verma.

Director Verma was a stickler for being reported to and Sean always followed the necessary orders.

Ch 14

In her bedroom, seated cross legged, her face scrubbed, her hair tied in a ponytail, and Sheena began downloading the search engine for Bollywood actress Aruna Shah.

She found a few short write ups and interviews given by the actress.

She made detailed notes in her file about all pertinent details.

She found the actress had no face book page but had an Instagram account. She had forty thousand followers and the page was strewn with pictures of her. In all she looked beautiful and every inch the Bollywood actress that she was. However, most of the photos were of her posing alone, but there were few of her in various functions like weddings and award ceremonies. She was photographed with various different men who apparently were her date for that evening. It was a known fact that she was single and so far there were no links with any man except the usual rumours about some affairs with married Bollywood actors.

She seemed a very elusive person where her personal life was concerned. In her interviews when questioned about her rumoured love affairs she maintained a tight- lipped silence using the standard phrase-"No comment."

As for her personal life regarding her childhood, it was merely stated that her parents were middle- class people- her father a bank cashier and her mother a housewife. She had a sibling, a sister a few years elder to her. But the name of her sister was not given nor were any details.

Sheena noticed in one interview given three months ago, she seemed very tight-lipped talking about her family.

She was asked by a popular talk show host about her family. She merely said, "My parents are dead."

When the talk show host asked her about her elder sister, she said, "She is dead too."

Her face had not been very relaxed. Most people might not have noticed this but Sheena had a sharp antennae for observing minute details. She noticed the wary look in her countenance as the camera zoomed on her expressive pretty face.

She made a note of this.

The next morning at breakfast with Sean, she told him about all she had discovered.

Sean thought for a long moment "Some celebrities are tight-lipped about family members. After all they are the stars. They wish to shield their family members. But let's explore this sister angle a bit more. It will come to nothing perhaps but we have to…"

"Examine every loose end." Sheena finished his sentence with a smile.

Sean gave her the thumbs up, happy she was looking better this morning.

Sean decided to quickly find out about Aruna's sister and then forget about it if they discovered it lead to nothing.

In order to do this, they had to visit the family residence of Aruna Shah where Aruna had resided before she became a Bollywood actress.

In order to do this, they had a lead. Aruna had stated in an old interview that the family had resided in Dombivli west, in a one bedroom flat.

Sean and Sheena knew she had also said they lived at 33rd street.

Thus, it would be easy to find her residence and chat with the neighbours.

So both set off with Alok at the wheel.

Ch 15

Dombivli is a city located near Mumbai in the Thane district of the Maharashtra state. The language here is officially Marathi but most people spoke other languages too based on their culture.

The distance from Thane to Dombivli was around twenty five km.

From Mumbai to Dombivli took them longer than two hours mainly be case of the traffic.

They reached 33rd street and told Alok to wait at the corner. He did so happily, fishing out his mobile to keep himself occupied.

They were unsure about her actual residence for the street was long and many small buildings stood there. They were not in the upper middle class category of buildings for most had a rather simple, plain appearance. None of the buildings had security guards.

Sean and Sheena walked around, their eyes sizing up the locality. Perhaps at one time it had looked more decent when the buildings had been new, but at present, they were unpainted and looked badly in need of renovation.

"From rags to riches, huh? Aruna Shah sure came a long way." Sheena murmured.

At one corner, stood a small shop selling various grocery items. The man was old and walked feebly.

Sean went up to him and asked him for a packet of digestive biscuits that he spotted at the counter. He was feeling a bit hungry and he also wanted more information about Aruna Shah.

The old man slowly removed the packet and handed it over.

Sean paid him the money.

Then Sean asked casually, "Is this not the same street Bollywood actress Aruna Shah lived in?"

At this, the man's face brightened.

He nodded, "Yes, same street." He looked very proud now as if by knowing Aruna Shah he had climbed up some kind of social ladder.

Sean asked, "I guess you know her, don't you?"

The old man nodded, "My name is Bipin Rao. I had this shop for thirty years. I knew Aruna as a child. Very cute thing, always coming to my shop for orange stick ice-cream. She loved it, you know. Polite, well- behaved, not like the kids today. They show no respect but she called me Uncle and always had respect."

Sheena asked him for an orange ice- cream stick.

He went to the small freezer and rummaged in it. Then he shook his head, "No orange stick, only chocolate."

"Will do" Sheena said quickly.

After paying him, they both lingered at the shop.

Sean began to open his biscuit packet and eat a digestive biscuit as if he was hungry, "Came all the way from Mumbai to meet a friend."

"Yeah, Mumbai is a long way from Dombivli. I never go there now. Too old to travel." said Bipin Rao.

Sheena asked, "Which building did Aruna live in?"

Bipin took his time answering, "She lived in Sai Raj, on the first floor. I know because I could view her flat from my shop. Always saw her mother hanging out wet clothes to dry in the balcony. They were a nice family, a bit reserved but polite people." He pointed out to an old faded cream building at the left hand corner adjacent to his shop.

"And today she is a big star!" Sheena pretended to be awed.

Bipin seemed happy at the attention he was receiving. He looked like a lonely man who craved company and attention.

He said chattily, "Yes, she is a star. I saw one of her movies. Odd thing to see a kid you knew well so grown up and becoming such a star. It feels a bit unreal. To me she is just little sweet Aruna who loved ice-cream."

"So she was the only child?" Sheena asked, taking her time to lick the stick of chocolate ice-cream that had a centre of chocolate laced with nuts.

"No, she had an elder sister." He frowned, "What was her name? Let me think. My memory is not what it used to be. Age, you know."

He thought for a minute, scratching his head. "Well, she rarely came to my shop that elder sister. She was at least eight years elder to Aruna, you now. There was a big age gap between the sisters. Okay, now I remember." He clicked his fingers, clearly enjoying himself. One got the impression he was a lonely man and enjoyed some company.

He said, "Nidhi, yes, her name was Nidhi."

 "She must have been similar in looks to Aruna. Bollywood must have missed another star. Pity she died." Sean said sympathetically, keeping his voice casual.

Bipin darted a swift look, the kind of look that told Sean that he badly wanted to gossip but he was pretending to be reluctant to come across as a gossipy kind of person.

He hesitated but admitted, "Yes, she looked a bit like Aruna and looked very nice. The two girls were the prettiest girls of this neighbourhood. She died I know. Actually, it was suicide." His tone lowered.

Sean darted a swift look at Sheena who was now placing the ice-cream wrapper and stick in the stainless steel bin next to his shop.

Bipin now, was clearly enjoying himself. He felt happy to be the centre of attention. Had he known the two were police officers, it was doubtful, he might have been so much at ease. The fact was seeing a lady especially an attractive one, most men relaxed because few attractive ladies in their eyes were detectives or cops. So Sean found worming information from people could be easier with Sheena by his side.

"She killed herself, very sad." The old man made a sympathetic noise.

Sean listened.

Bipin continued, "Most folks here said it was an unhappy love affair." He paused.

He lowered his voice, injecting a sombre quality to it, "Well, it was not a love affair, I think it was a lot more than that. The parents refused to divulge any information. They just let folks talk."

He said a bit triumphantly, "But I know something most people do not."

Sean did not speak now, he just listened.

Sheena stood by his side, the recorder on but the old man had no way of knowing his voice was being recorded.

He shrugged," No, I must not gossip." Yet the look on his face clearly revealed he was dying to gossip.

He said, "You want some cakes? My old lady bakes them, very nice. Mawa cakes and chocolate cakes."

Sheena took the bait. She said enthusiastically, "I love cakes. Let me see them."

Bipin reached out for the cakes placed in the counter below. The cakes were neatly wrapped in clear plastic. They looked appetising and smelt good.

Sheena looked at them, asked the price and then took two cakes, a mawa cake and a chocolate sponge cake.

Bipin looked happy.

Sheena then asked, "I wish you would tell us why the sister committed suicide. We promise not to breathe a word to anyone. We are not news reporters, you know."

 Bipin shrugged, "But no use raking up old stories."

But Sheena was not put off, "True, but perhaps your theory of why she died may be true of course, but it may be false too. Maybe that is why you cannot tell us. You don't know for sure."

Bipin frowned. He realised Sheena was deriding him and he did not like it.

He said brusquely, "I have work to do."

Sheena said cajolingly, "Okay, maybe we are too nosey, you know but you just got us interested, that's all. We mean no harm."

Bipin looked at Sean, "Your lady here is persistent. Why do you want to know?" Now suspicion laced his tone.

Sean shrugged, "My lady likes a bit of gossip. You now women, always reading Stardust and liking Bollywood actors. Indian women like Bollywood actors, you know that. She reads Stardust cover to cover. Aruna Shah is her favourite actress."

Sheena smiled, "I have two posters of Aruna Shah in my home. I like her. Any gossip about her interests me. I wish I could get her autograph. Maybe she comes here, huh? Just to see you."

Bipin made a face, "No, not once. But she is a star, why would she remember us? She is too big for us now."

 "Yeah, you got a point, once these people become stars, they forget the little people." Sean said provocatively.

Bipin rose to the bait. He seemed upset at this. He grimaced, "True."

Sheena began to put the cakes sitting on the counter in her shoulder bag. She carried a shoulder bag at times especially when they wanted to talk to people and not reveal they were police cops. People tended to ease up with normal looking ladies.

Bipin watched her with a dark look on his face.

He murmured, "Odd now Aruna thinks she may be too much but when her sister, Nidhi died, the whole family was the talk of the locality. "

Sean just listened. It did appear that at last perhaps the old man would unburden himself. He was carrying some information that he had probably never told anybody.

 "Nidhi was trying to become an actress, you know. Few people know this around here. If they do, they thought it was a fantasy all young girls have.

But I know it was a fact." He said quietly, his eyes at a distance. "You see, two weeks before she committed suicide, she came to my shop. She rarely ever came here so I was surprised."

He paused then continued, "Well, I asked her why she was looking so happy. She told me a film producer wanted to meet her. He promised her he would make her a Bollywood actress. She told me it was a secret. She had only told Aruna not even her parents. She swore me to secrecy and promised me a box of sweets if she got her first starring role."

He shrugged, "I half believed her. I mean these young girls, she must have been about twenty or so, and they say anything to get attention. I even suspected that she was a bit of a fibber, the kind who lies to get attention. So I just played along and told her that I would be waiting for the sweets. But a week later, she committed suicide. "

Sean glanced at Sheena and Sheena did not interrupt him.

Bipin continued, "So I tell you it must have not been a love affair, perhaps she was rejected by this Bollywood guy and so died. The parents did not reveal the autopsy report, all we knew was she had hung herself from their bedroom ceiling fan with her dupatta."

Sean realised that the old man was telling the truth. He looked sincere enough.

Sensing he had nothing more to say, Sean was quiet. Just then another customer, a middle-aged lady came to the shop.

They both left the shop saying goodbye to him. Bipin was now busy with his new customer who was asking for washing powder and he seemed to forget about them.

Ch 16

On the way home, Sean said, "This loose end is worth pursuing. I think there is a lot more to the story than we understand. We got to pursue this."

Sheena nodded, "Yes, I think we must."

When they got back, they found on the internet an article from a popular newspaper written more than ten years ago. It dealt with the suicide of Nidhi Shah from Dombivli who had committed suicide. It stated she was the eldest sibling. Her parents were middle-class. The police had no idea why she did so because her parents too seemed totally bewildered. The autopsy report was kept private. It appeared the police would be dismissing it as a case of suicide. The victim had left no suicide note behind. Murder was ruled out because according to the forensic pathologist, it did appear that she had taken her own life. There were no fingerprints of any strangers except for the family members in the bedroom.

The picture of the deceased was a pretty young girl with a lovely smile. She looked a bit similar to Aruna except Aruna was far prettier.

They checked subsequent newspapers for the story but it appeared the newspapers had dismissed it as a case of suicide and since it was not murder, the police were not interested in investigating it.

Sean sat still for a long moment, his mind evaluating facts. He was trained to sniff out the scent of a likely suspect or a likely reason for murder.

He said slowly, "Here we may just may have a possible reason for murder and revenge. Nidhi was most likely approached or had approached a Bollywood person who had promised her stardom. What are the chances that she met Karan Desai?"

Sheena asked curiously, "Do you think Aruna is the most likely suspect now?"

Sean said, "We have to tie up all the loose ends, fit the jigsaw pieces in their place. This is an important piece of the puzzle. We would be fools to ignore this."

He thought hard and said, "I will call Pranoy Roy."

Sheena watched him as he soon got Pranoy on the phone.

Pranoy luckily was at home, and seemed free to talk.

Sean said, "Would you by chance have heard of an actress or rather an aspiring actress by the name of Nidhi Shah?"

 Pranoy Roy said, "No...don't think so."

Sean said patiently, "You might not remember but she knew Karan and had met him regarding some movie he promised her. She looked a bit like Aruna." It was a wild shot. He winked at Sheena as he spoke when he noticed her bewildered expression.

Pranoy was silent, then he said, "Well, I remember a young girl whom Karan had introduced me to in his office. I mean the guy saw many would be actresses. But if my memory serves me right, she was pretty and was different from the others. She had a kind of naivety and innocence. Funny she looked a lot like...."

He suddenly stopped.

Sean filled in, "Like Aruna Shah, right?"

Pranoy was cautious. He said warily, "Perhaps. I mean she looked a bit like Aruna but......"

"She was offered a role by Karan? Sean asked, diverting the subject.

Pranoy said, "I do not know. I mean, I just saw her twice in his office, yes, it was around Diwali time I remember. I had gone to meet him regarding some vacation I had planned and wanted a few days off from shooting. He had agreed and my assistant stepped in my place. I remember Nidhi. As I said she looked innocent and that kind of struck me. Bollywood is a jungle, innocent damsels get eaten up!" He chuckled a bit at his own witticism.

His voice was guarded now, "What has this got to do with the case?"

Sean said, "We are police officers, we ask the questions."

His voice was a bit curt.

Pranoy fell silent.

Sean then said more kindly, "Look, did you see Nidhi after this?"

Pranoy shook his head, "I was on vacation and when I came back, we flew to Singapore for shooting. Karan was with us there. He wanted to be in the thick of things."

"Did you know that Nidhi died shortly after this? It was suicide."

Pranoy was shocked, "Really? I had no idea. I never heard this. Was it in the newspapers? Because I rarely read newspapers. I just watch the television news channel, that's all. It's a bad habit, I know but that is my style. I do not think any mention was made on the television news channel."

"Yeah, those channels will report celebrity deaths but it was in the newspapers."

Pranoy said, "I see."

Sean said, "Do not talk about our conversation to anyone. This is strictly between us."

His voice brooked no argument.

Pranoy said swiftly, "Of course, of course. I will be the soul of discretion."

Then Sean thanked him for his time and switched off the mobile. He looked at Sheena, "I think the pieces are falling into place."

Sheena agreed.

Ch 17

Director Verma was appraised of the facts. He said, "Watch these Bollywood types. We have to be careful. "

Sean said, "Yes, we will be. But I need to bring in Aruna Shah for questioning."

Director Verma agreed, "But be prudent. She is a Bollywood star. She will want her lawyer if you harass her."

But before they did so, Sean went to Aruna's residence and spoke to the building manager. He asked for security footage for the month of June. It was now August.

The building manager, an elderly stout man said, "I will check. It should be available."

He went into his office and Sean and Sheena followed him.

He took a while and then called them to view the security footage that the CCTV cameras had recorded for the months of June to August. Both were given chairs to sit on. The building manager then excused himself and told them he would be back in an hour.

Sean and Sheena peered at the screen.

They spotted Aruna Shah getting in her chauffeur driven car at least twenty times in the month of June.

She seemed to lack any visitors.

Sean zoomed on the screen.

There were no CCTV cameras in the lobby of the flats on each floor except the building area. She had no visitors except her daily maid. However, on June 15th a young man had come to see her. They knew this was probably a visitor because he took the lift to the floor she resided on. Most likely he had come to visit her yet he could also have been a visitor to any of the other two flats on the same floor. The time was eleven in the morning. He had in his hand a package. He looked tall and quite attractive. He was dressed in jeans and a light blue shirt. Sean decided to call the security guards.

Two of them entered, looking a bit nervous as most did when faced with cops.

It was confirmed that the young man had come to see Aruna Shah. He had been permitted to go up after the security guard had confirmed it was okay by Aruna Shah after speaking to her on the intercom.

The two guards then left.

Sean said reflectively, "Something tells me that this guy could have answers. We got to find him first before talking to Aruna. He is a loose end and I need to tie up this loose end before we talk to Aruna."

Sheena agreed. She had the same gut feeling.

Ch 18

To find out who he was proved to be easy because he had written his name on the guest register.

He had used the name Satish Tiwari and had signed the register too.

It took a while to track him down but they managed to do so after a day's work of inquiry.

He resided in the same area, in fact three buildings adjacent to Aruna's residence.

They met him at his workplace which happened to be an industrial laboratory around a mile away from his residence.

He came to meet them after his manager informed him that the cops needed to talk to him.

He looked slightly nervous but that could be expected of anyone who had to talk to cops. Few people looked very self-assured meeting cops.

They met him in the manager's office. The manager was asked to wait outside.

Then Sheena shut the door.

The air-conditioner was on and it dispelled the heat of the morning quite effectively.

Satish was told to be seated which he did.

Sean asked him his full name. He replied, "Satish, Satish Tiwari." He was asked his designation in this work place.

He said, "I work as a laboratory research assistant to Doctor Ranade. I have been working here for five years."

Sean asked, "What is your relationship with Aruna Shah?"

Satish looked a bit startled but he said quickly, "Aruna? You mean the Bollywood actress? Ah, she was an old friend of mine. I have not met her in a while."

Sean asked, "When was the last time you saw her?"

Satish shrugged, "Maybe a year ago. I cannot say."

Sean said, "But the CCTV cameras clearly show us your presence at her building on June fifteenth. Do you deny that?"

Satish looked shocked. He never expected this.

He stammered, "I don't...'

Sean said pleasantly, "Would you like us to show you the footage? You went to Aruna Shah's home that day."

Satish admitted it, "Perhaps but we know each other. Why should I not visit her?"

"Then why the hell did you lie? You said you had not seen her for a year."

Satish looked at his feet.

Sean stated, "You held a package in your hand."

Satish shrugged, "Well, maybe. It was a gift for her."

Sean said, "What was the gift?"

Satish looked away. He said a bit sullenly, "It was a perfume for her."

"Really? I think it was not perfume."

Satish looked at him, a wary look in his dark eyes.

Sean said, "I think it was a bottle of cyanide stolen from this laboratory."

Satish stared at him, fear creeping in his eyes.

He denied it, "No, it was not cyanide."

But his voice lacked real conviction.

Sean said, "Look, you better tell us the truth. If you co-operate, we will see your sentence for abetting murder will be reduced. You will get bail. I promise you this. Just help us here."

Satish wrung his hands and he muttered, "Why did I get involved? Why?"

Sean waited, knowing he would soon crack. He was a bit of the nervous type. Sean could see that being on the wrong side of the law would never sit well with him.

He said, "Alright. I will tell you everything." He appeared keen on unburdening himself. One got the feeling he had detested his role in the crime.

He began, "I knew Aruna and her sister Nidhi. We were in the same school. We were not the best of friends but we got along well. Once we even went on a group picnic together."

He paused then continued, "But Nidhi committed suicide. I was shocked. The whole locality was shocked. No one knew why. Not even me. But few months ago, Aruna met me. She was jogging around the local park. I went there every morning for a walk and sometimes I used the exercise equipment in the park. Well, we met. We talked a bit. After this, we met at least once a week. It was a Saturday I remember. She seemed depressed. I cajoled her to tell me what upset her. And then she told me how Nidhi, her elder sister had been raped. Raped by Karan Desai, the Bollywood producer. I was shocked. Aruna told me that the day before she died, Nidhi had told her how she had trusted Karan and had met him through a friend of hers. The friend had been in her college and her dad had invited Karan to a party because her dad had been musician for

Bollywood films. He played the guitar. So they met and Karan seemed impressed by her. He invited her to his office to talk about her chances in Bollywood. Nidhi wanted to be an actress. Even in school and college she used to act in the plays. Everyone thought she did a fine job. So Aruna told me how Karan raped her in his office. She had been devastated for he had also told her he did not think she was good enough for Bollywood. She was very devastated. All her dreams went to ashes."

He paused, "Aruna did not tell her parents because she knew how upset they would have been and besides she always planned to take her revenge one day on Karan. She told me that Nidhi made her swear not to tell anyone. She was too ashamed. The fact was that Nidhi was very conservative. She wanted to become an actress only because of her talent. She was very strait-laced. Not the type meant for the casting couch. She really believed that talent was enough. She was a bit naïve. If her parents had known about her meeting Karan Desai, they would have objected because they were the type who thought good girls got married and had kids. Nothing more. So Nidhi blamed herself too much. Maybe if she had support, she might have not done this. But Aruna was younger than her and I think Aruna was always regarded as the baby of the family, so Nidhi did not count on her support. "

Satish paused. He looked very distraught, "I shifted from Dombivli here because my job was close by. My present flat is rented. I was happy to stay close to Aruna."

He sighed, "Aruna wanted revenge. She knew I worked in an industrial laboratory. She asked me for cyanide. She had done her research on it. I was shocked and refused. But she begged me to get it for her. I told her that I wanted no part in this. If she wanted cyanide, she would get it but I did not want to hear why she wanted it. I knew I cared for her and knew she was desperate. She was crying a lot and I comforted her. So a week later or so, I brought the cyanide to her residence. I left quickly. I knew she was bent on revenge. Then I heard about the death of Karan Desai. I knew what she had done."

He buried his face in his hands.

He muttered, "I meant no harm. She asked me to. How could I refuse?"

Sean said grimly," Well, you must come with us to the police station."

Satish obeyed. He put up no resistance.

Ch 19

Aruna Shah was asked to the police station in South Mumbai.

She was a bit reluctant and insisted on her lawyer being present.

But Sean told her that first they would interview her alone then she could summon her lawyer.

She agreed reluctantly but had little choice.

In the interrogation room, Sean and Sheena interrogated Aruna Shah. Inspector Bose watched from the room behind the two way mirror.

Aruna Shah sat ramrod straight, her expression cool. She looked beautiful as always, however the tenseness around her mouth detracted from her lively beauty.

Sean began the interrogation asking her if she had anything to do with the demise of Karan Desai.

She bristled and said coldly, "Nothing whatsoever. I am innocent."

Sean then asked her, "Have you ever seen cyanide?"

Aruna was quick to deny this, "Of course not. I have no reason to see it. I did Commerce in college. I am not a Science student. I do know that cyanide is poisonous but that is all."

"So you never touched a cyanide bottle?' Sean asked.

Aruna said, "No."

Sheena questioned, "Are you acquainted with a man named Satish Tiwari?"

Aruna looked startled, but she recovered quickly. She was not an actress for nothing.

She said, "Yes, we were in school together. He resides in my locality. I do not see what he has to do with my interrogation." She made it seem as if her time was precious and they certainly were wasting it!

Sheena questioned coolly, "Are you denying that Satish Tiwari visited your residence on June fifteenth and handed you a package. That package contained a bottle of cyanide from his industrial laboratory."

There was a shocked look on Aruna's face. Suddenly she did not appear so cool and beautiful but looked like a cornered rat, her face tight, her eyes frightened.
"This is bullshit! I want my lawyer. You cannot deny me the presence of my lawyer. I refuse to be browbeaten like a common criminal."

Sean rasped, "Madam, kindly compose yourself. You will get your lawyer but first answer the questions please."

Aruna was mute.

Sheena said, "We have the CCTV footage, you know, of Satish visiting you with the package of cyanide. He had admitted it to us."

Aruna said, "No, this is untrue. He gave me a package but it was not cyanide. It was a gift."

Sean said, "Ma'am, he has confessed. A bottle of cyanide is missing from the laboratory. Dr Ranade in charge told me this. We have obtained a search warrant for your home. You will wait here while we search your home."

Aruna went wild, "You have no right. This is outrageous. I will complain about you. I am a Bollywood actress, I have my rights!"

Sean said coldly, "Ma'am you could be the Prime Minister for all I care. The law is the law. Justice is for everyone."

 Aruna bit her lip and looked away.

Ch 20

With the search warrant, the officers searched Aruna Shah's residence. Her maid sat in the kitchen looking as if the world had come to an end.

After an hour, one of the constables showed Sean a small white label that had been torn off from something. It read **Cyanide,** with the poison sign on it. The bottle was not to be found. It was surmised that Aruna on receiving the bottle had torn off the label and it had fallen on the ground, tossed a bit by the wind from the big opposite windows, under the dressing table. The maid had not swept it away luckily.

"Thank goodness for maids who do not always sweep under furniture often enough." Sean murmured.

But they could not find the cyanide bottle. It was concluded that Aruna had discarded the bottle perhaps not in her vicinity. But they were not sure.

When Aruna was confronted by this evidence, she broke down and began to cry.

 All her cool composure vanished.

Sean said grimly, "I can understand your need for revenge because your sister died, but one cannot kill someone and play God."

Aruna confessed to them a few hours later. She looked wan and seemed to want to confess.

She said, "I loved my sister. Karan ruined her life. In fact, he ruined my family. My parents were never the same again. They were devastated and there was always depression in our home. I hated him. I wanted him to suffer. Without Nidhi, they had lost their hope and happiness." She buried her head in her hands and sobbed.

She told them, "When the others were staring at the beautiful lady in the painting, I moved away and pretended to look at the other paintings. I crossed the room and had to pass Karan's glass. Quickly I opened my purse and put the poison in. The whole thing took two minutes. Fortunately nobody noticed, not even Sarika because she was looking at some painting of water lilies. The bottle I later discarded in the bushes along my street. Karan had no right to rape Nidhi. He thought she was fair game. He must have realised she was innocent and not wealthy and thought nothing to taking advantage of her."

Aruna Shah was led away by the constables. She looked forlorn and defeated.

Director Verma sent an e mail to them – *Good job. Your flight has been booked for tomorrow morning.*

As the aeroplane flew across the blue sunny skies, Sheena murmured, "Sometimes the killer gets my sympathy."

Sean nodded in assent, "Yeah, me too. Let's hope Aruna gets a lighter sentence."

Months later, newspapers carried the report that the presiding judge, Judge Haresh Saini, a secret fan of Aruna Shah, had sentenced Aruna to ten years imprisonment with every chance of parole for good behaviour. It appeared the court was sympathetic to her need for justice for her sister.

When Aruna Shah was released after three years on the grounds of good behaviour, to everyone's surprise, she was offered a role in a Bollywood film based on her crime story. It was a hit and Aruna Shah was once more a Bollywood star. The forgiving public soon welcomed her back. In many ways she was a bit of a heroine, a young woman who took revenge to honour her innocent sister. It was the stuff Bollywood movies were sometimes made of.

Story 3

The Swami of Enlightenment

Ch 1

Sean was sitting on an armchair in his balcony, enjoying his morning tea in his small bachelor studio apartment. He had bought it a few years ago.

It was cosy and easy to maintain. A maid came in the mornings at six to clean and left just half an hour later.

The time was now seven and he was due at work at eight. Since it was just a twenty minute drive, he generally left for work at around seven-thirty.

The headlines in the newspaper caught his eye- **Swami Laxman, the Swami of Enlightenment found murdered at his ashram in Thane.**

He read with interest how the Swami was found with his head bashed in the ashram.

The photo was not very clear but since it was black and white, the bloodied bashed head could not be viewed clearly. It was stated that he was found in the morning around six by his followers who tried to revive him but finding that he was beyond help, they summoned the police.

According to the medical examiner's report, death took place between mid-night and two o'clock in the morning.

The body, it was reported was sent for post-mortem and the Thane police were investigating the case.

So far there were no suspects. Robbery was suspected but so far nothing was found stolen but investigations were on.

A week later

Sean and Sheena were summoned to Director General Verma's office.

Sheena on their way together murmured, "I think I know which case wants us to solve."

Sean said, "The murder of the politician's son?"

Sheena shook her head, "No, I think it's the Swami case."

Sean then remembered reading about Swami Laxman. He had been murdered in his room at the ashram in Thane.

He said, "Maybe you are right."

Director General Verma's assistant Mohini, was seated in a mini cabin adjacent to his own. It had an open door and she could view people clearly. Seated in front of her lap-top, she looked up as they approached.

She was dressed in a pink kurta and black pants with a pink dupatta cowl style. She was young in her twenties but efficient. She stood up and led them to his office. The door was open.

"Sir, the officers have arrived."

Director General Verma looked up from the paperwork on his polished teak desk and said, "Do come in."

They both entered and sat down opposite him on the straight backed chairs. They were not designed to be comfortable. Mohini left and quietly shut the door.

Director General took off his black rimmed reading glasses. He looked at them and said, "A new case has come up. It is in all the newspapers. It has generated its fair share of interest."

He paused and looked at them, "It is the murder of Swami Laxman. In fact there are some of his you tube videos around and you can look at them. He preaches on a better spiritual and happier way of life. He was nicknamed the Swami of Enlightenment. He became a popular man."

Director General put his hands on his desk, entwining his fingers, a gesture he often used when he was serious about something. "He was conducting a course on Enlightenment in Modern Times, at least that was what his followers told the cops at Thane. But on the tenth day, his body was found in his room, his head bashed from a big hard rock lying beside him. Apparently the rock was from a flower-bed in the vicinity. He put up no sign of struggle because there were no injuries on his body so most likely the perpetrator took him by complete surprise. It seemed like a pre-meditated murder yet we know little. The Thane police have not made much progress. Since this is a bit of a high profile case, some pressure has been put to get quick results. And that is where you two- The Express Squad come in. You are to fly today evening to Mumbai and then a hired cab will take you to Thane. This time we are not putting both of you in the Andheri guest house. Instead you will use a hotel that is near the ashram in Thane. Two rooms have been booked for you. The hotel owner, Mohinder Singh knows you are police officers and he has accommodated other CBI police officers before. The car with Alok will be available to you."

He paused and looked at them, "Any questions?"

Sheena said, "Sir, we would like to tackle this case. I have been following it intently."

Director General Verma smiled, "Good, then I shall expect quicker results."

Sean nodded," Well, I hope so. We shall do our best."

Director General said, "Mohini will give you your flight tickets. I want you both to leave and pack. The time now is eleven in the morning and the flight is at five this evening. Be at the airport at three o'clock latest."

They both stood up.

Director Verma said, "You know the protocol. Inspector Kumar of the Thane police who was handling the case will talk to you about it and give you the files. You will work in co-operation with him."

"Yes sir." They said respectfully in unison and left the office.

 Mohini with a smile, handed them the two flight tickets.

She murmured, "Good luck!"

Taking the flight tickets, they left for their homes, eager to pack. Every time they worked on a new case, it felt exciting like an adventure though a bit stressful because the pressure to solve it was quite high.

Ch 2

After reaching Mumbai, they were whisked away in a prepaid taxi to Thane. The journey was long and it took them close to two hours especially since the traffic was heavy.

Sheena sighed, "Travelling can be killing at times. I feel tired given the heat."

In Mumbai there was a heat wave and the temperature had soared to thirty- eight degrees.

Fortunately, the cab was air-conditioned and Sheena felt measurably better.

Sean flicked through his mobile for e mails and messages.

Both were dressed casually in jeans and T shirts. No one looking at them could have guessed that they were CBI officers.

At last they reached Thane.

Thane, a metropolitan city in Maharashtra is situated in the north-eastern portion of the Salsette Island.

This city is the 15th most populated city in India.

Thane is also called the Lake City. It has 35 lakes in the city. The word Thane is derived from the local Marathi word Thane which means Police Check Post.

The Central Railway is an important means of transport in this city.

On reaching Thane, they were taken to a small hotel named, Cosy Haven, run by Mohinder Singh.

He was in the lobby when they entered the hotel. He seemed to expect them.

He greeted them politely and instructed one of his waiters to carry their luggage to the third floor. The hotel had just four floors.

It was well-maintained though, not luxurious. The floor was granite and there were potted plants in the lobby. It seemed aimed at middle- class customers and seemed to promise a cosy and enjoyable stay.

They used the small lift that took them up to the third floor.

The red carpeted floor gave a clean vibe and their rooms were opposite each other.

The waiter opened the hotel doors with a set of keys.

Mohinder Singh watched as they entered the rooms saying, "If you need anything, please ask the front desk using the intercom in your rooms."

The view was good from both the rooms for the hotel overlooked a small lake.

Mohinder Singh said, "This hotel so far has housed four CBI officers in the past. I do hope you both have a good stay. Here is my mobile number."

Both saved his mobile number on their phone.

He then left with a smile.

He seemed an affable man and depicted characteristics most people associated with those working in the hospitality industry such as politeness, cheerfulness and a certain poised calmness. He appeared like the type that little would hassle him.

Both unpacked and decided to meet in the small hotel restaurant for dinner.

The dinner would be paid by their office and they were free to order as they chose. The only rule was no alcohol would be paid for and generally it was taken for granted that they should not consume alcohol on the job. They both followed rules diligently.

Both had a quick hot shower and dressed in fresh pressed clothes.

Sheena looked cool and comfortable in black jeans and a cropped green top.

Sean looked equally casual in black jeans and a white casual cotton shirt that he had not tucked in.

His hair was lightly damp.

The restaurant was at a far end on the ground floor. It looked neat and clean.

The tables and chairs were made of cane and had red and white table cloths.

There were paintings on the walls depicting landscapes and rural scenes.

There was also a big map of Thane on one wall, with pictures of important Thane residents who had frequented the hotel at some point of time.

There was music playing from the loudspeakers. The vibe was cosy and pleasant.

"I like it." Sheena said, looking around appreciatively, "Yeah, not bad. Guess it makes a change from the Andheri guest house."

"Yes, guess so." Sean agreed.

It was decided by both that the next morning they would visit the Thane police station and meet Inspector Kumar.

According to a message they both received from the CBI office in Delhi, Inspector Kumar was apparently expecting them.

After a light dinner followed by a fruit salad topped with fresh cream and jelly, they went back to their rooms, feeling tired and caught a good night's sleep

Ch3

Inspector Kumar greeted them politely.

He seemed a bit tense as if he felt a bit inadequate for not solving the case although only a week had passed since the death of Swami Laxman. After the introductions had been made, a peon came with a tray of three cups of hot piping tea.

They sipped the tea slowly while Inspector Kumar filled them in with the case. He seemed an articulate man who liked to talk.

He said, "It is a case which we felt we could solve but happy you guys are here. So far there are no clues and it could be just anyone. I mean, there were thirty people in the ashram listening to him preach each day. Fifteen were men and fifteen were women. But so far all seemed normal people, most from middle- backgrounds and a few very wealthy folks. All of them seem innocent but obviously someone had to be responsible. Actually we have two major suspects. One is a middle-aged gentleman who had a fight with the Swami regarding the fees and donations just a day before the murder, the other is a young woman who was openly sceptical about the preaching of the Swami. She had stood up during his preaching and told him he was talking nonsense. It did not go well with some of the others who began to quarrel with her. She told him she wanted to leave and wanted her money back. The Swami told her to be calm and not to get upset but she flounced off. The next day he was murdered. So we have two major suspects. However, it could be someone from outside. The ashram is situated in a rather deserted area. It is situated away from the main city next to a small village. Anyone could have entered. The worst thing is that no CCTV cameras were installed. His bodyguard used to function as a caretaker of the ashram. It was a very rustic kind of atmosphere. I mean the man used to conduct his preaching under a huge pipal tree in the garden. The followers had to sit cross-legged on mats and listen to him. I guess to them he was a kind of semi-god. When he was found murdered, he was clad in black shorts and a vest."

Sean listened. He then asked if the names and addresses of the main suspects were in the case file.

Inspector Kumar replied in the affirmative.

Inspector Kumar called the constable and told him to fetch the murder weapon. The constable returned a minute later with a plastic bag that contained a black rock. Inspector Kumar showed them the rock that was used to murder Swami Laxman. It bore faint traces of blood. It looked lethal enough to either badly injure someone or kill them.

Sheena said, "We will also question the staff. I guess there were staff?"

Inspector Kumar nodded, "Yes, there was a cook, an assistant and three male servants who worked as cleaners. Also there was a gardener and of course his bodyguard."

"We cannot rule anybody out." Sheena stated.

Inspector Kumar agreed.

They then took their leave, promising to keep Inspector Kumar appraised of their investigation.

When they left, Sub- Inspector Pai joined Inspector Kumar, "Think they will crack the case?"

Inspector Kumar shrugged, "These two have got a rep, a reputation of being the Express Squad. They are fast workers. Got a feeling they will crack the case."

Sub-Inspector Pai said, "Yeah, hope so."

And that was that. Inspector Kumar now turned his attention to the pressing case of an artist found dead in his home last night. His man servant was absconding. He would have to leave with his team to go to Bhopal, the native residence of the manservant.

Ch 4

At four-thirty that evening, Sean and Sheena set off in the car with Alok driving. He had been given a room in the hotel on the first floor, a cheaper smaller room but he seemed happy enough.

He said, "I have never been to Thane. Nice place. Better than I expected."

"It has certainly developed." Sheena commented as the car sped through the streets lined with towering attractive buildings, many had recently been developed.

The ashram was situated at the outskirts of the main town and it took them almost forty minutes to reach there.

At present it bore a rather forlorn look. But some of the followers were still at the ashram, others had left after the murder.

Sean and Sheena parked in a special place reserved for visitor's cars. Alok waited patiently in the car.

They noticed that the grounds were fairly big. There was a small garden at one corner with shorn grass and trees lining the edge. There were benches for seating and a small fountain of an apsara in the middle gushing water.

The rest of the grounds were cemented. They entered the garden.

Sean noticed the flower bed in the small garden that was laced with big black rocks. He bent down and picked up one of the black rocks. It was almost identical to the murder weapon. However, at a corner there was a rock missing. That rock had been the murder weapon and at the police station.

Sean and Sheena had gone through the autopsy report prior to their visit here.

The autopsy report had stated that Swami Laxman had been killed by a very hard object that had been used repeatedly, like an act of passionate rage.

Swami Laxman had not been a big man. He had been hit on the back of his head a few times. He had not been facing his attacker when he had been attacked and it probably took him unawares for there were no signs of struggle. Death had been instantaneous. He had fallen to the ground, and perhaps had not viewed his attacker full face.

Now, as Sean studied one of the rocks carefully, he realised while it was heavy, in the hands of a slim person filled with rage it was very possible use the heavy rock without feeling its weight too much for it was not big, merely medium sized.

He placed it down, his eyes surveying the landscape carefully. He was then met by Mohan, the caretaker who looked a bit distraught. He was a big man both in height and bulk. He had served as a caretaker and body guard for the Swami.

Sean asked him to lead them to the ashram building.

The walk from the flower bed to the ashram building took two minutes as Sean had estimated.

The building was a small one. The ground floor had a big open space used for lectures and seminars.

At the left hand was a big bedroom that was the Swami's bedroom. Mohan led them there, opening the latched door. It was austerely furnished with a single bed, cotton grey curtains on the big windows and had a small wooden wardrobe.

There was a tiny attached bathroom that had a washbasin with an oval mirror.

The look was a bit austere. Mohan said, "This was where the Swami stayed, his living quarters. He shunned any form of luxuries."

Sean said, "You were his bodyguard, right?"

Mohan nodded.

"But where were you on the night that he was killed?"

Mohan sighed, "That evening I had been exhausted because I had gone to town shopping and I was fast asleep in my cabin. I blame myself." He looked away, his face distraught. Either he was a very good actor or he really was sincere.

Sean said, "What kind of security measures were taken here?"

Mohan sighed, "Not much. The Swami was a bit lax when it came to security. He always thought God would look after him."

Mohan shrugged, "But it was not to be." He looked bitter.

Sean prodded, "What about at night?"

Mohan said, "Well, the front entrance door was locked but the Swami's bedroom door was latched from the inside. However, he always slept with the windows open. He liked fresh air. I told him to install grills but he just laughed. He should have listened."

Sheena asked, "What about money? Did he keep cash here?"

She went to the wooden wardrobe and examined it. It contained only three white cotton kurtas and two pairs of trousers. It had few white vests and few black shorts neatly folded that he used for nightwear according to Mohan. There were two pairs of average sized white underwear and one pair of black socks. At the bottom were two pairs of sandals.

There were two razors on a top shelf and nothing else.

She closed the wardrobe.

Sean went over to the big open window whose curtains were drawn.

He pulled open the curtains and peered outside.

The ground was cemented outside and it bore no trace of footprints. The traces of mud found on the rock according to the forensic report were from the garden.

Since the door had been found to be bolted when his body had been discovered, it was obvious that the killer had come in through the window. There were chances that if the Swami knew the attacker, he could have opened the door for him or her, then after the murder, the killer escaped through the open window, bolting the door.

Sean jumped outside and found it was very easy to do so. Even a child could jump out of the window without hurting itself.

He surveyed the cemented pathway.

It now looked clean and the traces of mud that had been there had been taken for forensic examination by the pathologist who had stated that the mud was from the garden. So obviously the killer's shoes had left traces of mud on the cemented pathway directly below his window.

The window had been dusted for finger-prints and six sets of fingerprints had been obtained. Few days ago before the Swami had begun the course in the ashram, some workers had been called to fix the window panes of the window. The window panes had been cracked and needed fixing.

The fingerprints of the two major suspects who had quarrelled with the Swami had been taken but they did not match the fingerprints found on the windows. The worker's fingerprints had been fed into the computer but they found no match of any person with a police record or on the wanted list. It would be hard to trace all the workers since they were migrant workers who had come to stay to do some odd jobs in the locality and each one had gone to his respective native place. They had been employed by the Swami who wanted to help them with employment.

Yet, the fingerprints found in the room by forensics might not be of the assailant but just a person who was not connected to the crime for the Swami had received some followers in his room at times. If the assailant had worn gloves, then the fingerprints obtained would be of little use.

Sean then jumped from the window in the bedroom.

The rock used to murder the Swami had been found in the room lying next to his body.

Sean looked around.

Sheena strode into the bathroom. She looked around.

There was a towel rack at a corner. On it was a green big towel hanging.

She removed it and found a grey underwear with a band around it that read- *Mufti-* it was a small brand that manufactured underwear.

She looked at the underwear that looked average size. Sean joined her and he too examined it but shrugged as if it was not important. Sheena placed it back in its original position.

Sean and she then moved out of the room.

Ch 5

The first suspect in Inspector Kumar's eyes was an elderly man named Sunil Dighe.

He was a man who seemed very opinionated.

The Swami's flock stayed on the first and second floor.

They stayed in big dormitories. The men stayed on the first floor and the women on the second floor.

Sean and Sheena met him in the men's dormitory. The other members had gone either for a walk or they had gone into town. The dormitory had several beds. There was a big bathroom at one corner.

Sunil Dighe was alone, sitting on the bed, reading a small book.

He seemed upset at their need to question him but relented rather reluctantly.

He said, "I want to leave here but the Thane police have instructed us to stay for another week, then we can leave. This is most upsetting. I am a bachelor but that does not mean I have to stay here."

 Sean reassured him, "After the interrogation done by us in a few days all of you may leave. Anyway the course was for thirty days and you paid for thirty days so enjoy the free meals."

Sunil Dighe said accusingly, "Some women, five of them were allowed to leave. Why us? Are we suspects?"

Sean said, "Two were elderly with heart problems and three were pregnant. They were allowed to leave for obvious reasons."

Sheena said, "The total number of you was thirty, now it is twenty-five."

Sunil Dighe said, "One of us is a young man working in the kitchen."

“Really? Who is he?”

“Some young man that suddenly joined the group. I heard he comes from the village. His mother works as an assistant helper to the cook in the kitchen. The Swami allowed him to stay here with us.” Sunil Dighe looked disgusted, “He is just the son of a staff member. He should not be allowed to reside with us.” His snobbish nature was apparent.

“Why did you quarrel with Swami Laxman?’ Sean asked. Both Sean and Sheena sat on chairs they had pulled up next to his bed.

Dighe snorted, “He was okay, what I mean was that he preached to us nothing new. He asked for heavy fees. On top of it we had to donate to his ashram, a big sum to show our solidarity for him. I gave the man fifty thousand rupees as a donation. We got simple food here and these simple accommodation quarters. I felt we were being cheated. The Swami talked a lot about austerity, simple living. I got cheesed off.”

Sean questioned, “Did you threaten him?”

Dighe shook his head, “No, I did not. Just made a few points of dissatisfaction that was all. People around me got upset and began to tell me that the Swami was God’s chosen one and I should pipe down. “

Sheena asked, “What made you change your mind about him?”

 Dighe’s eyes shifted. He said sullenly, “I think he was a fraud. I paid good money for all the tripe he spoke about. Clean living, healthy eating, arranging one’s home according to Vastu Shastra which tells you the traditional system of bringing luck and prosperity something like Feng Shui the Chinese believe in. He spoke about spiritual oneness with the Creator etc. I was bored. I know all this. What was new? I paid good money for all this.”

It was clear the issue he was most concerned about was the money.

Then the two left after ascertaining there was nothing more to be learnt.

Sean, on their way up the flight of stairs to the women’s dormitory said thoughtfully, “I think he seems okay but we cannot rule him out as a suspect.”

They reached the second floor.

Ch 6

It was similar to the first floor with the same layout.

There was a big open space that served as a dormitory with several beds and a big bathroom at one corner.

Five women had been permitted to leave the ashram.

Ten women were there chatting, some doing embroidery, some just lying down. One was mediating solemnly, on the floor. No mobiles were permitted. Their mobiles were left at home.

Sean asked for Rohini Sapre. The meditating elderly woman seemed oblivious to their presence. She had opened her eyes just once, glanced at them and continued meditating.

A petite slender young lady raised her hand.

She looked bolder than the rest. Her hair was cut short in a longish pixie cut. She was attractive and looked intelligent.

Sean introduced Sheena and himself and told her to come outside because they wanted to talk to her.

She stood up and accompanied them.

Sean led her to a small room on the third floor that served as a library. It had rows of shelves that housed many books. They looked in decent condition.

There were tables and chairs. The members were free to read any book when they chose.

He gestured her to be seated.

She sat down gracefully.

Sean asked her about the quarrel she had with Swami Laxman.

Rohini smiled slightly as if she found it a bit amusing.

She said, "All I did was to point out something in his talks that did not jell with me. I mean he was preaching about vastu and how we must arrange our homes in a particular manner. I stood up and argued that this was foolish and we must trust in God rather than silly things like whether the furniture should be to the right or left. The Swami was calm but I knew he got riled. He then gave us big lecture on how this was a traditional science that proved accurate. I argued that nothing could be proved in a laboratory except a few silly examples given by people who had experienced good or bad luck. It was like a superstition I said, if one arranged furniture and got bad luck, one thought the placement was to blame. If this happened more than a few times to different people, it was now written in stone. I told him this was rubbish. The others got upset with me for daring to challenge his teachings. I was fed up and wanted to leave. I mean I am a spiritual person but I am practical too. But the next day he was murdered."

Sean sad, "Have you visited the bedroom of the Swami?"

 Rohini shook he head, "No, not me. Never seen his room. Is it grand or simple?" She looked very curious.

Sean replied shortly, "Simple."

Rohini smiled, "I am kind of sick of this place, you know. I want to go home. All this austerity and simple living bores me."

Sheena asked, "So what made you come here? You must have known an ashram was like this."

Rohini sighed, "Believe it or not, I was going through a breakup. My boyfriend left me. It was a tough period and my aunt recommended coming here because I was a bit upset. But I regret it because all this crap.....I mean the murder, happened. Funny enough, I recovered from the breakup. I actually met someone here."

Sean asked quickly, "Who?"

Rohini blushed, "His name is Rohit Chitnis. He is a software engineer. He came here because his uncle recommended this course since he had left his job and was looking for new employment and was at home. We hit off."

Sean said, "We would like to talk to him."

Rohini nodded, "Sure, he should be back, he went to town to buy some goodies for me to snack on."

She heard a car in the driveway. "Think it could be him. He was the only one who took the car out today, the rest went for walks or took public transport."

 A few minutes later, they heard footsteps and a man of medium height with fine straight hair cut in a fashionable style, dressed in jeans and a casual blue shirt came into the library on the third floor.

There were no restrictions about the sexes intermingling when the Swami had been alive, but it was a rule that men could not visit the women's dormitory without permission from him.

He looked surprised seeing them here. He had a book in his hand.

"Just returning it." he said.

There was no librarian in the library. One could just walk in and take any book off the shelves.

He walked to the third shelf and put the book back on the shelf carefully. Then joined them as Sean said, "We would like to talk to you."

Sean introduced Sheena and himself and asked Rohit to be seated.

He looked a bit surprised, hesitated but complied. He pulled up a chair and sat beside Rohini.

She touched his hand briefly, a sign of comfort. He looked at her and there was a softening in his gaze. "I bought some snacks for you."

"Thanks." She smiled at him.

Sean cleared his throat and asked, "Was it a shock when the Swami was murdered?"

Rohit looked surprised, "Yes, it was."

Sean said, "Let me rephrase that. You see the Swami could have enemies. In fact, Rohini herself quarrelled with him and threatened to leave. Mr Dighe too had issues about the fees and the donations. So there could be plenty of folks who might bear a grudge."

Rohit took his time to answer. One could imagine the wheels of his brain turning. He was a man who was not impulsive but rather analytical.

He said, "Yes, what you say has truth in it. Whenever a person tries to be important or gather public interest, he can come in for a fair share of criticism. This hold true especially when money is involved. People may get resentful."
Rohini took offence. She butted in, "It was not the money, I just...."

Rohit was firm with her, "I am talking to the Inspector now. Please do not interrupt."

Rohini shut her mouth. She looked away, her mouth sulky.

Sean suppressed a smile. Rohit certainly could handle the bold, impulsive Rohini.

Rohit, was now clearly enjoying himself. He continued, "So yes, he could have made enemies and someone killed him. I do not think it was robbery because nothing was missing in the way of cash and the Swami never kept jewellery in his room or anything of value."

Sheena piped in quickly, "How do you know this?"

Rohit shrugged, "The Swami made it a point to tell us this on the first day. He was a clever chap, he told us he believed in austerity and simple living. I guess he was afraid of robberies and made it clear he had nothing of value."

Both the Inspectors nodded as Rohini said, "Yes, that is true."

"The men are on the first floor. Did you hear anything that night?" Sean asked, looking searchingly at the other man.

Rohit thought a bit. He chose his words, "Well, the Swami's room is on the ground floor but if you viewed it, it was at the furthest end of the floor. So we are not directly below him. Besides he was hit on his head when his back was turned. I mean I read about this in the newspapers. Maybe he hardly had time to scream, the blow took him by surprise. So we would not have heard anything."

Sean raised his eyebrows a bit. Rohit was an astute man.

After some more questioning, it became apparent neither had more to offer in terms of information.

Rohini could not help having the last word, "Funny, is it not? For all his preaching and spirituality, he could not be saved."

Rohit shot her a chiding look, "Never speak ill of the dead."

Rohini made a face and shut her mouth.

Sheena looked a bit amused.

Then, both left.

Sean asked, "Your input?"

Sheena shrugged, "A perfect match those two."

Sean had to laugh.

Ch7

They decided to speak to the kitchen staff and the cleaners.

The staff's quarters were about a few yards away from the main building. It was newly painted and looked neat and clean.

The kitchen was big and there was a lady dressed in a cream sari who was cooking. Another middle-aged lady clad in a blue sari was chopping onions.

Sean and Sheena introduced themselves.

Both the women looked a bit daunted but that was to be expected.

Sean and Sheena told them to continue cooking and they would chat with them.

The two women looked at each other and nodded deferentially.

Sean tackled the lady wearing the cream sari.

He asked, "Your name and designation?"

The lady stirring the big pot said, "Mala Shetty. I am the cook. I have served here for the last five years. I come from Bihar and the Swami gave me this place to stay. I also help to clean the place. I am a widow but my son works in the village as a farmer."

The village she was referring to was adjacent to the ashram, around only half a mile away.

Sean asked the blue sari clad lady chopping onions the same question.

The lady looked up and said, "My name is Parvati Patil. I, too, come from the village. My husband died a year ago and the Swami gave me this job as an assistant to the cook. I live here but sometimes go back home too."

Sean asked, "Whose son resides with the others?"

Mala Shetty pointed out to Parvati, "Her son, Gopal."

Parvati put down the chopping knife and began to knead some dough.

Sean asked her, "Why did the Swami permit your son to attend the course?"

Parvati shrugged, "My son Gopal is educated. He completed his schooling three years ago. He was looking for a job and the Swami told him to work as his assistant. But first the Swami told him to attend this course and learn his preaching. So Gopal was allowed to stay in the dormitory. But now lately he is living at the village. He has found a job helping a farmer but comes here too to assist me."

Sean said, "I would like to talk to him."

Parvati said, "Alright, I will call him." She picked up her mobile and called her son.

After a minute, she said, "He will be here in fifteen minutes. The village is a ten minute walk from here."

Sean asked Mala, "Did you see or hear anything on the day Swami Laxman was killed?"

Mala Shetty stopped stirring the big pot and said, "Sir, we stay here in the quarters close to this kitchen. There is a big room for us. The men sleep in the next room to us. That night it was hot and I stood outside at the doorstep. I remember that it was a full moon night. I did not see anything suspicious. It was around eleven. Then I went back to sleep. The Swami was murdered later, I know but I saw nothing nor heard anything."

Sean looked at Parvati, "What about you? Did you see or hear anything?"

 Parvati shook her head, "Both of us shared the same room. We saw nothing."

Just then the gardener, Vikram and the cleaners, Parth, Sourav and Raju came in. They had come into the big kitchen to eat their lunch. There were small chairs with tables in the kitchen for the staff to eat.

Sean questioned them but they said that they neither saw nor heard anything.

They claimed they had worked in the ashram since it had begun. It appeared they were loyal servants for they seemed sincere.

In fact, they looked tearful as if they were very distraught by his demise.

Just then a young man lad of around seventeen strode in. Parvati raised her eyes from the rotis she was rolling out and said, "This is my son, Gopal."

The boy was around five feet five or so. He had straight raven hair that looked oiled. He had a tanned complexion and he was not very lean. He had a rather good physique. He was good looking and seemed nervous. But that was to be expected.

Sean told him to sit down on the chair.

He did so. He was wearing faded jeans and a blue T shirt.

Sean and Sheena sat opposite him.

He looked his hands nervously.

Sean said kindly, "We only want to ask you a few questions. Just relax, okay?"

The boy looked up. Sean noticed that his eyes seemed very intense. His eyelashes were thick and so dark that the bottom eyelid appeared as if he had use kohl pencil to underline it.

He was truly an attractive lad.

Sean asked him first his name, age and residence.

He said, "Gopal Patil. I am seventeen years old, my birthday was last month. I live in the Suraj village with my mother. She lives here at times. I used to live here for a few months when the Swami stayed here."

"I see. Why did the Swami ask you to attend the course?"

The boy's eyes shifted slightly. He chose his words carefully, "I had finished my grade ten and was helping a farmer with his work. But the farmer suddenly died. I had come to the ashram to help my mother with the cleaning of the kitchen because she had been unwell and I washed the dishes and swept the kitchen. I used to assist her in the kitchen, you know peeling the potatoes etc. The Swami saw me and he called me to talk to me. I told him I had just completed my schooling. He told me he would give me a job as his assistant. He would pay well. He promised me a salary of ten thousand rupees. I was very happy. I asked mum and she agreed. The Swami told me that he wanted me to attend the course. It was a thirty day course. He said it would help me to understand his work and also educate me about spiritual life. I agreed. I resided with the others in the men's dormitory."

Sean listened.

Sheena asked, "Did you hear or see anything that was suspicious that night?"

Gopal shrugged, "I did not hear anything. I am quite a deep sleeper."

"What is your opinion about the murder? Perhaps you have a theory?' Sheena asked, with an encouraging look.

Gopal stared at his hands. He seemed thoughtful, then he shrugged, "I really cannot say. I think he must have had some enemies or somebody wanted to rob him."

Sean asked, "You have no idea at all?"

Gopal nodded, looking a bit relieved, "No, honestly."

Sean nodded. The questioning was at its end. He knew he would get no further information from the boy.

"You may leave."

The boy got up and he then spoke to his mother.

It was obvious that there was deep bond between mother and son.

Then Gopal stood next to her, helping her to chop the tomatoes for the meal.

Sean and Sheena left then, convinced that lingering on would yield no benefits.

Ch 8

At dinner at the restaurant of the hotel, Sean asked Sheena, "Tell me what you have surmised?"

Sheena helped herself to pasta and topped it with Milanese sauce which was laden with broccoli and oyster mushrooms.

"This is pure Italian. Heavenly!" Sheena murmured appreciatively, after the first bite.

Sean watched her, an amused look in his eyes. Sheena had a good appetite yet remained remarkably slim, her athletic figure always attracting interest.

She then looked at him, her eyes serious, "See, this is incredible that no one saw or heard anything. Either we are dealing with the perpetrator who is one of these people here or a total stranger. My bet is...." She paused and her brow was knitted in a frown. Then she said, "I think it is very likely one of these people. No robbery had been committed. So money seems not to be an issue. But it could be possible that the intruder thought the money would be in the Swami's room. But the Swami was not asleep and the intruder attacked him. The intruder found no money. However, the contents of the room were neat. It did not look like any rummaging was done to find money. The wardrobe was neatly arranged. The intruder seemed not to be in a hurry if he opened the wardrobe and this does not jell with the theory that the act of murder was committed in either anger or fear of discovery. I would most likely say the killer was a known person to the Swami."

Sean listened. He always thought Sheena made good observations and her input was always valuable.

She merely was voicing all that was on his mind. He had drawn the same conclusions.

He said, "We have to then pay more attention to the people at the ashram. We have to adopt the policy that no one is above suspicion. Everyone is suspect. We have to talk to them again and spend time at the ashram. Someone out there may know more than they are revealing. Someone who may have seen something or knows something that they are not revealing, either because of fear or because they do not know the information may be important. You know what mean. People see or hear important things but they pass it off as unimportant not realising it may be a vital clue. It happens often enough but it also can help solve a case."

Sheena agreed, "True."

Sheena looked a bit tired. Sean noticed her sleepy face.

"Tired?"

Sheena smiled, "A bit."

Sean said, "A pity. After dinner I wanted to propose a walk in the garden. It's a nice garden here, not big but decent and well- maintained."

Sheena said quietly, "Sounds nice."

Sean looked at her in surprise. He had not expected her to agree.

They both decided not to have dessert although they could have their pick of ice-creams and black forest cake which was the specialty of the day.

Together they made their way outside. It was cemented but had a small pretty lawn with benches at a corner. There was a small fountain in the centre gushing water into a small pond filled with colourful fish. Both of them spent a few minutes looking at the pretty sight. There were colourful stones lining the tiny pond and the fish darted around happily.

"It's pretty!" Sheena commented.

"Yeah, nice."

Sheena went towards a tall coconut tree whose branches were gently waving in the breeze.

She leant on its thick bark.

Sean looked up at the tall tree and said, "There are many coconuts. One could fall on your head."

Sheena smiled, "Yes, but I am taking my chances."

"In a dangerous mood?" Sean teased.

The atmosphere between them was light.

Sheena felt the cool breeze dispel the heat of the day.

She leant against the tree, her eyes surveying the vicinity." It is so peaceful here. Sometimes I wish……" Her voice trailed off.

Sean looked at her curiously, "Yes, go on."

Sheena shook her head, looking a bit discomfited for her reserve had thawed. She wished to maintain a professional air with him. It was too dangerous not to because the attraction between them was potent.

But Sean was persistent for he moved closer, "Go on, tell me. Sometimes baring your soul helps."

Sheena laughed, "No, it's nothing. All I was thinking about was that our jobs deal with so much violence, crime, despair, pain…… so life seems to be so negative. Standing here I feel as if there is so much beauty in life, so much goodness and life seems tranquil. But it's all an illusion. Our work only shows us life is bitter and dark."

Sean thought for a moment, "Yeah, it is true. But solving cases is positive. Life has its yin and yang- the good and the bad, the beautiful and the ugly. The opposites exist side by side. So it is not just our job, it's the world in general that is two faced."

Sheena countered, "But we see the ugly mostly, don't we? How much of beauty do we see? Theft, murder, rape…….it's ugly."

Sean said," You seem in an introspective mood."

Sheena sighed.

In the evening shadows, despite her tiredness, he thought that she looked lovely. His eyes fell on her soft pink lips and the urge to kiss her almost overwhelmed him. He had to restrain himself with some effort.

As if sensing his thoughts, her eyes swirled to his face and their eyes met. It felt as if time stood still.

He wanted to look away but the vulnerability on her face made him quite unable to tear his eyes away.

There was no invitation in her eyes, only a kind of helpless inevitability that made him realise that she would not object to a kiss.

He moved closer to her and she stood still. He gently bent down and brushed his lips tenderly against her lips. She shut her eyes and he intensified the pressure on her soft inviting lips.

She moaned a bit and they kissed passionately as if at last they had been gifted an outlet. She entwined her arms around him and he drew her closer, their bodies striving for further contact. There was something so warm and comforting about his embrace. It made her feel warm and protected. Loved and cherished.

After her divorce she had tried dating. Her friend, Palak, had set her up with some guys. But all the dates had been disastrous because she had not found any of them attractive enough or interesting enough. Her job had also been a kind of turn off to them once they understood it well enough. They felt she would not make good wife material. Two of the three men had tried to get her into bed. But she had spurned their advances. Needless to say, all three never attempted to contact her again. In their eyes she was not easy prey nor potential long term relationship material.

She had decided to engross herself in her work. But these days the joy of her job was diminishing. She found herself staring enviously at married couples and even enviously at mothers with their offspring.

She did not comprehend the change in her. She did not want to face it but bury her head in the sand.

Now Sean was eliciting responses from her that frightened her.

Sean drew back slightly, his eyes taking in her flushed face.

Gently, he caressed her face and said, "You are tired. You better go to bed."

Sheena flushed, feeling a bit ashamed.

Sean looked at her and said, "You do not know how hard it for me to say goodnight. But we have to obey rules."

Rules meant no romance between detectives on the job. She knew this.

Mutely she walked with him.

At the door of her room, she turned to him and murmured, "Goodnight."

"Sweet dreams." he said, his eyes lingering on her face, yet his self-control was admirable. He did not want to jeopardise their jobs, especially hers. She could land into a lot of trouble. He knew most likely Director Verma would blame her for being feminine and weak to indulge in romance.

It was often a man's world in their field. Women detectives were few and Sheena had to prove her worth. It had been a hard climb but after working with Sean Fernandez, she was being taken more seriously, especially after the success they had. Yet there had been male colleagues who had hinted it had been Sean who was the true detective in their team. It was untrue but this was the kind of bias she faced. You had to be tough and Sheena was tough but not so tough that she did not get hurt or develop a hard demeanour. Her face still had that was femininely soft allure that was attractive to a male.

Both went into their respective rooms and shut the door.

Ch 9

Rohini and Rohit walked around the ashram grounds. The sparrows chirped noisily on the tall trees, flitting about busily.

Rohini said pensively, "We will be permitted to go home tomorrow. They cannot force us to stay here."

Rohit said, "Yeah, but it was a nice course. Very disappointing that it came to an abrupt halt."

Rohini shrugged, "Thought the Swami was a bit of a…."

Rohit shot a look at her, "What? A fraud?

Rohini said, "Well, not completely but a bit of a mountebank, a charlatan."

Rohit was quiet. He did not share the same views.
Rohini understood this but her personality was such that often other people's feelings did not always matter. She prided herself on her common sense and logic.

They came towards the garden. Rohini hesitated. Rohit looked at her, "What's wrong?"

Rohini shuddered, "The weapon was a rock from this garden. I cannot walk here without feeling upset. "

Rohit said, "C'mon. There is no need to be so frightened. The garden has no killer now."

Rohini looked at him, "Are you sure?"

There was a subtle change in her tone that made Rohit frown. "What are you saying?"

Rohini hesitated, then shook her head.

Rohit halted and now they were facing each other.

Rohini looked away.

"Tell me what is on your mind."

Rohini sighed, "Nothing."

But the stubborn look on Rohit's face made her decide to be upfront with him. Besides, she was hardly a shrinking violet.

"Okay. The fact was on the night the Swami was murdered I saw you out of my window."

Rohit looked startled, "What!"

Rohini asked, "Do you deny it?"

Rohit looked at her and he seemed uncomfortable, "I do not know what you are talking about."

Rohini countered, "Really! I am sure I did not imagine seeing you at eleven going for a walk."

Rohit said, "Okay, maybe I went for a walk. There is nothing wrong with that." He said angrily, "What were you doing at that time? Peering out of your window?"

Rohini flushed, "Actually, I had gone to drink water from the filter next to the window. As I was sipping the water, I saw you were walking towards the garden."

Rohit shrugged, "Yeah, that day I was feeling a bit restless and wanted to walk about. Could not get sleep. Nothing wrong with that."

Rohini said reflectively, "The Swami was murdered between mid-night and two o'clock, wasn't he?"

Rohit stared at her in consternation, "Yes, so are you accusing me!"

Rohini asked, "Have you told those two detectives about this?"

Rohit looked distinctly uncomfortable. He looked away.

Rohini said quietly, "I think you must tell them or else they might suspect you."

Rohit muttered, "No one else saw me but you."

Rohini looked at him and said, "So you will not tell them. Why? If you have nothing to hide....."

Rohit glared at her, "You know you are so bloody bossy. I think I will go back now. Goodbye."

He strode away.

Rohini stared after him, gaping a bit.

Then thoughtfully she too, set out in the direction of the ashram.

Ch10

Rohini realised that Rohit could be stubborn. If he decided to do something, then he would. He did not wish to tell the police officers about his walk that night.

She pondered over this. She liked Rohit but no way was she going to have a relationship with someone who was acting secretive. She decided she would tell the police officers. Besides, he was now not talking to her and her one attempt to talk to him was met with stony silence. The next day they were all to leave.

So she rang up Sean whose mobile number she had and told him about Rohit's walk that night of the murder.

Sean thanked her. He had Rohit's number and called him up.

Rohit seemed upset when Sean told him that he wanted to talk to him.

But he relented.

Half an hour later, both of them were at the ashram. Rohit was in the library as they had requested.

He was seated on a chair and he looked angry. There was a scowl on his attractive face.

Sean and Sheena sat opposite him.

He burst out angrily, "This is Rohini's interference, right? She spoke to you. I could wring her neck…"

Sean looked at him with raised eyebrows, "You have a temper, don't you?"

"Yeah, so what? Rohini had to open her mouth."

Sheena looked at her long fingers carefully, measuring her words, "What are you upset about? You went for a walk on the night of the murder and you never told us about it. This is concealing vital evidence, you know. You can be accused of perjury. You never told us you went for a walk on the night of the murder. What time did you go out and what time did you return?"

Rohit said sullenly, "Believe it or not, it escaped my mind."

Sheena looked sceptical, "That is hard to believe especially given the fact that you are very upset and are also refusing to talk to Rohini."

Rohit said, "She accused me. She thinks I did it. But all I did was to go for a bloody walk. That night it was hot and I felt like having some fresh air. So I walked outside, nothing more to it."

"Did you go into the garden?" Sean questioned.

"Well, yes but just for a while. I returned at around mid-night. I know this because I glanced at the clock at the entrance. Nothing wrong with a walk. But I knew the police would find it suspicious. Can you blame me for not revealing this? Just see how you are now suspicious of me." His voice was a bit bitter.

Sean said, "Yes, but you should have lent us your full co-operation while questioning. This does not look good for you."

Rohit said, "So what are going to do? Arrest me? I did nothing but take a walk."

"If you are innocent, then help us out. You must have seen or heard something that night. After all the Swami was murdered between mid-night and two o'clock." Sean stared at him intently.

Rohit looked at his clasped hands on the table. He sighed, "The fact was I never saw or heard anything. The place was deserted and everyone was in the ashram. I saw Mohan, the bodyguard and caretaker in his cabin. But he was fast asleep. He did not see me. His cabin is a yard away from the ashram. That day I knew he had gone into town and he had arrived late. He was tired, I guess. But I saw no one around, I swear."

Sean and Sheena looked closely but there was just sincerity in his face. It was hard to believe that he was lying.

Sean said, "Next time you are questioned, I would advise you to tell the truth. It saves time and you do not look guilty. Now even if we believe you, you are now our suspect. We will be keeping a close eye on you. I know tomorrow all of you will be leaving. You better give me your home address. We might talk to you again."

Rohit did so, his face unhappy.

Sheena said, "Rohini contacted us because she felt that hiding things might get you into trouble. Someone like Mohan could have seen you so I think she thought it is better that you are honest with us, especially if you are innocent. If you are innocent then she will be happy. Rohini is smart and if I was in her place perhaps I might have done the same thing. No lady wants to be with someone who may be guilty of murder. I think she has honesty in her and that's a good quality, one that has to be appreciated."

Rohit looked at her and he sighed, "I guess you are right. It's just that I just want to return home and get on with my life. I have a job interview coming up and don't want to jeopardise my career because of one stupid evening walk."

Rohit insisted that did not see or hear anything suspicious and that he was innocent. They had no evidence so they had to let him go.

When he had left, Sean asked Sheena "Do you think that he is guilty?"

Sheena said, "Hard to say but perhaps not. But we will keep him on our lists of suspects for now. After all everyone is guilty till proved innocent."

"Right." Sean stood up and both made their way down below.

Ch11

Mohan was in his cabin, flicking through his mobile, looking a bit bored.

He straightened up seeing the two officers.

The cabin was small but comfortable and a small fan twirled around at a corner offering respite from the heat.

As a bodyguard, of the Swami he was also a security guard of the ashram and a caretaker. He said sadly, "I had been exhausted on that fatal night. I blame myself sometimes. This ashram property was rented and the owner is in America. He wants us to vacate as soon as the lease is up which is in three months. So I can stay here and then all of us will leave and look for other jobs. "

The unhappiness on his face was apparent.

Realising he had nothing more to say, both of them left, walking around the premises.

Sheena said, "Someone has got to know something. Suggest we talk to the others group wise at least and find out if anyone has something to say."

Sean agreed.

Both of them went up to the men's dormitory first. On the way up there was a small wooden cupboard that seemed open.

Sean opened it and found it had bed linen. The bed linen looked washed and pressed. Everything was arranged neatly in piles from the white pillowcases to the bed sheets and the fluffy blankets for the colder months. There were moth balls placed at strategic points. It was kept for the residents to use when needed. Sean shut the cupboard finding nothing of great interest.

The men's dormitory was filled with the few men chatting. All were present except for Gopal Patil.

Sean and Sheena decided to adopt a casual approach.

They sat on the chairs next to the beds.

Sean said, "I know that tomorrow you will be leaving here. Since this is the last meeting here, we thought of taking a bit of your time and have a kind of group discussion."

Dighe was the first to respond, "What exactly does a group discussion entail?"

It was clear he was a bit of a feisty man always ready to argue.

Sean said patiently, "Just want a bit of feedback. You are intelligent people and we think you might offer good insights that sometimes we may not see."

This appeared to be the right tactic because not only did Dighe look mollified but the others too looked in a more co-operative frame of mind.

Sean asked, "All of you are aware the Swami was killed between mid-night and two the next morning. Now he slept on the ground floor and you sleep on the first floor. Now we think someone must have heard something. After all he was murdered, his head bashed with a hard rock."

There was a murmur amongst the men.

Sheena asked suddenly, "Where is Gopal?"

Dighe answered promptly, "He stays in the village and comes to help his mother. He no longer resides here." He looked happy at that prospect as if he could not bear the hired help fraternising with them.

"I see" Sheena said.

One of the elderly men, a gentleman named Haresh Pawar said, "You know the room of the Swami was not directly below us. It was on the ground floor at the far end. Also according to the newspaper reports, the Swami was not facing his attacker. His back was turned. So one blow was enough to stun him and he would not have cried out for it would have taken him by surprise. It would not be surprising then, that we heard nothing. I think it was a pre-meditated attack because the killer had brought the rock with him and wanted to kill him. "

Dighe retorted a bit rudely, "What is new? We all know that."

Sean looked at Haresh Pawar and said, "Your insight is correct."

Haresh flushed, looking pleased.

A tall bespectacled man named Prem Ahuja said thoughtfully, "I think that Swami Laxman had an enemy since money was not taken. In fact there was no money in the room. Apparently, I heard that the Swami always used his credit or debit card in the ashram and never carried money. So it was a crime of passion- hate and revenge. Maybe his teachings infuriated someone enough to murder him."

Dighe butted in, "Nonsense! I think that someone must have thought there would be money and killed him."

Prem Ahuja pointed out, "But the room was not ransacked. Everything looked neat and orderly."

Dighe flushed, "Perhaps the killer is too clever. He must have known nobody would come at that time of the night to the Swami's room. After killing him, he must have carefully looked through the room. He must have tried not to awaken anyone and been quiet. He must have not wanted it to look like robbery."

"Bah!" Prem Ahuja said rudely. "You would make a third rate cop!"

Dighe flushed. Suspecting that a quarrel might break out, Sheena said quickly, "Anyone else has any insight? For example on that day did you see any stranger lurking about or anyone acted suspiciously?"

The men looked at each other and no one seemed to know what to say.

They seemed clueless, glancing at her bemusedly. Sensing that they would not get information easily Sean looked at Rohit and said pointedly, "You left the dormitory for a walk."

Rohit flushed. He nodded.

All the men's eyes swirled towards him. Some stared at him almost accusingly.

Rohit put up his hands, "Hey, don't look at me like that as if I was the killer. Can't a guy go for a walk? It was innocent, I swear it."

Dighe stared at him, "You did not tell us about your innocent walk that night." His voice was sarcastic.

Rohit said, "It was none of anybody's business."

The men now seemed uncomfortable.

Sean said, "So you see, none of you saw Rohit leave. I presume that all of you were fast asleep. Suppose somebody else left, then you all would say they never saw him leave. Get my point? Obviously, someone amongst you left the dormitory that night besides Rohit, presuming he is innocent."

Haresh piped in, "What about the ladies? They could be guilty too. What about the staff members?"

All the men agreed loudly, "Why accuse only us?"

Sean raised his right hand, "Okay, point taken. But you must understand that if none of you saw Rohit leave that night, then the killer might have left the dormitory but none of you saw or heard him leave."

Prem said, "Point taken. But we did not see anyone leave. I think that most of us were tired. You see the whole day we had been listening to talks by the Swami. It started at around eight that morning we were given a light breakfast and it continued till one. Then after lunch we had to attend another lecture that went on for two hours. After that, all of us were led by the Swami around the ashram. He made us sit in a quiet spot in the garden next to the fountain and meditate for an hour. That was a long time. I felt bone tired. Then we had our dinner at seven after freshening up. So you see all of us were tired. "

Rohit said, "That's the point. When I get mentally fatigued, I feel like moving about. I could not sleep that night so I decided to go for a walk in the garden. "

The men still looked at him a bit suspiciously. He flushed.

After this, realising that they would get no more information, the two decided to pay a visit to the women's dormitory on the second floor.

Ch 12

Fortunately, all the women were present except for the five who had been permitted to leave. They seemed excited returning home the next morning.

Rohini sat on her bed and looked a bit depressed.

Sean looking at her, guessed the reason why. Things were strained between her and Rohit. Rohini meant well but she had not reckoned with the stubbornness of Rohit. In actuality, Sean really thought that both of them made a good pair but were too thick headed to learn how to compromise. But he hoped they would, they kind of deserved one another.

Sean and Sheena told the ladies present that they were just asking them for their insight.

An elderly lady by the name of Sanjana Sharma said, "We are happy to leave tomorrow. It was not fair that we had to remain behind. Some ladies were allowed to leave."

Sean pointed out all fifteen of them had paid for the thirty day course and only five left because of health reasons. They were given comfortable accommodation and free meals. It was not so bad.

Sanjana made a face. It was clear that she was keen on going home as soon as possible.

In the room there were ten ladies of varying ages but Rohini was the youngest, the others were middle-aged or elderly.

Sheena said encouragingly, "I think you know that women compared to men are often very observant, they tend to notice small details. When we questioned the men, few knew anything much but we know you must have seen or heard things that they did not. So we want you to give us your observations, anything that you may have seen or heard that can shed light on the murder."

Sanjana piped in, "If you ask me, I think Dighe did it. That man is insufferably rude. He was so rude to Swami Laxman. And the other day he had the temerity to tell me that we were not educated enough to see that the Swami was a fraud. The nerve of the man! I suspect him."

Three of the other elderly ladies raised their hands in agreement.

Sheena suppressed a smile. She said briskly, "Okay, now that is your theory. But what we are looking for is facts- that is what your eyes have seen or your ears have heard. "

Sanjana said sagely, "A witness?"

Sheena nodded.

Sanjana shook her head, her eyes darting across the other ladies. They looked at her and did not seem to offer anything.

Rohini commented suddenly, "The fact was we were tired that day. It had been a particularly long session. I think we all fell fast asleep. Maybe the Swami was tired too and that is why he was not on the alert. The intruder must have taken him totally by surprise. Being fatigued from all that lecturing, he must have been too tired to do much. Besides he was struck from behind, so perhaps he never even saw the intruder." Rohini shuddered, "What an awful way to die!"

The other ladies present looked at each other, clucking their tongues sympathetically.

Sean took over, asking, "Perhaps you might have heard the Swami cry out?"

It was a shot in the dark.

But surprisingly one of the ladies said, "That night I was feeling thirsty around one o'clock. I was drinking water and stood in front of the window sipping it. There had been a full moon that night. It was not so dark and I could see the grounds of the ashram. For a moment my sleepy eyes thought that I had seen a movement near the flower bed with the hard rocks. The flower bushes are so big they conceal anybody unless the person is very tall. But suddenly at that moment, Sanjana here sleepily asked me what the matter was. I turned to her and told her that I was thirsty. She told me to go back to sleep. I put the glass down on the side-table and jumped into bed. I did not glance from the window again. But looking back, I guess the intruder must have been out there."

Rohini piped in, "It could not have been Rohit. He had gone for a walk but told us he returned at mid-night."

Sanjana pointed out, "He could have been lying."

Sean and Sheena listened.

Then after realising there was nothing concrete could be gauged from them, they left.

Ch 13

The next day

Sean and Sheena arrived at the ashram at eleven and found that most of the residents had left.

 Rohit and Rohini were in their respective dormitories.

Both seemed very depressed and were getting ready to leave.

Sean and Sheena spoke to them briefly, then walked around the ashram premises, meeting Mohan sitting in his cabin, looking a bit more cheerful.

He told them, "I am called for an interview tomorrow. A rich businessman from Thane wants me to serve as his driver and caretaker of his bungalow. The salary is good, better than I expected. I hope I get the job. My fingers are crossed."

Sheena smiled, "Best of luck!"

"I sure need it!" Mohan smiled back, suddenly looking younger. The depressed mood was gradually lifting away.

Sean said thoughtfully as they walked away from earshot, "It is odd, right? People mourn for themselves more than the person who died. They worry about their own misery."

Sheena nodded, "Human nature?"

"Yeah." Sean said, as they walked towards the staff quarters and kitchen.

Rohini climbed down the stairs with her red suitcase.

She walked slowly.

As she neared the men's dormitory, Rohit was also leaving with a big black shoulder bag. Their paths collided and he exclaimed, "Oops! Sorry!"

Rohini looked flustered and she bit her lip.

Rohit looked at her a bit coldly and then said, "So you are leaving just like me."

Rohini stood there feeling like her world was falling apart.

The truth was that she liked him a lot. She had enjoyed talking to him and enjoyed the chemistry they shared. But because of her big mouth, she probably had blown her chances.

She shuffled her feet, wishing she knew how to put things right. She felt tongue-tied, a feeling that was not very familiar to her. The sight of him made her heart thud faster and her longing for him intensified.

She said lamely, "Yes, I will be catching the bus. It will take me home. My home is in Seawoods Nerul, Navi Mumbai, so it is not really far away." Rohit who lived in Andheri, just nodded.

Rohini looked at her suitcase and said in a cheerful tone, "Well, it was nice meeting you."

Rohit's face had not softened. He looked angry as if he still bore resentment against her.

She said lamely, "Goodbye, then, I guess we will never meet again."

She felt her throat constrict. She longed for him to pull her into his arms and kiss her like he did before their fight. But his face was hard and implacable

She moved away quickly, before he could witness the surge of moisture in her eyes.

She had begun descending the steps to the ground floor. She heard his footsteps behind her but refrained from turning around. She had her pride.

As she reached the ground floor main entrance she heard his voice call out, "Rohini!"

She stood still, then slowly turned around, frightened what she would find on his face. Hate? Anger? But Rohit said gruffly, "Let me give you a ride home. I will be passing your way."

Rohini could not believe it. She hesitated and again his face grew hard, "Well, that was just a suggestion. I can see you suspect me."

The anger in his voice was apparent.

 "How can you say this? I admit at first I was upset because these last few days have been quite stressful what with the murder, the cops hovering about, questioning us like we are suspects. So I just thought that..."

"You thought I could have killed him." Rohit said bitterly.

Rohini said tremulously, "No, not really but yes, doubts crept in my mind. Also I felt it was wrong of you to conceal this. What if someone saw you? Like Mohan for example. Then the cops would suspect you at once. So I wanted to make a clean breast of things."

 He said, "Anyway whatever. So are you coming with me?"

Rohini this time did not hesitate, "Yes, thanks. Kind of you."

Rohit looked at her with an odd expression as if kindness had nothing to do with it. The fact was that he knew deep down that he was still attracted to her. He knew she felt the same, she was never very good at hiding her feelings.

They walked to his blue sedan.

As soon as Rohit started the ignition, the car roared off.

Ch 14

Sean and Sheena met Mohan who said, "All are gone except for the staff. Will leave in a week. I allowed them to stay here for a while. Most are looking for new employment."

Sheena looked at him, "What about you?"

"Well, the businessman offered me the job today. I met him an hour ago and he wants me to begin in a week's time because he is going out of town. So I will stay here and have to pay the staff. The Swami had left his credit card. The police had it because I told them where he had kept it. It was kept in a secret drawer in his cupboard. Only I knew about it because he trusted me. So I will pay the staff and then the police can have it back again."

"The Swami had no kin?" Sean asked.

Mohan said, "None that I know of. He had made a will that was found with his bank manager who had kept it in a bank locker for him. According to the will, he left all his money to an old age home in Thane. I know this because the police told me this."

Sean also knew this because Inspector Kumar had informed him of this fact a few days ago.

He nodded.

Mohan said sadly, "I will miss Swami Laxman. He was a good man."

There was nothing more to say. Both the officers moved away, leaving Mohan with his sad memories.

Rohit drove carefully along the streets. There was silence in the vehicle because both felt awkward about things.

Rohini gazed out of the car window, quite sightlessly.

She wondered whether she had blown her chances with Rohit. She and her big mouth!

Shucks! Why did she have to be so damn honest and sincere? But it was just her nature, like a dog's tail was either straight or curvy. You could not bend it much.

Rohit said after fifteen minutes of no conversation, "Rohini, I have been doing a lot of soul searching. I think you were partly right."

Swiftly her head turned and their eyes met.

He warned, "Mind you, not fully right but partly."

A glimmer of a smile touched her lips.

He looked at her and made a face, "Okay, laugh. But yeah, good thing the cops know about it. I had been feeling guilty about not telling them. You walked in and solved the problem."

Rohini smiled and said mockingly, "I deserve something for this."

"Name it." The flirting quality of his voice was apparent.

 His teasing made her feel bolder, "You owe me a kiss"

"Oh? Really?"

Rohini could not meet his dancing eyes.

Shyness overwhelmed her and by nature she was not a shy person. But Rohit aroused feelings that were new to her.

Abruptly Rohit halted the car at the side of a rather quiet street that led directly to the main junction.

He turned to her and his eyes fell on her lips. Her heart was beating so hard she was sure that he could hear. He bent down and brushed his lips against hers.

She responded and soon one kiss led to another.

Gently, she broke away and said contritely, "I am sorry if I hurt you."

Rohit caressed her cheek tenderly, "Not to worry. I think things worked out fine. I will reach you home now but I am looking forward to seeing you soon. This Saturday are you free?"

Rohini nodded, feeling excited and happy. "Yes."

He then kissed her gently and turning away, began the car.

Rohini smiled. Things were perking up. Definitely!

Ch 15

Making their way to the kitchen and the staff quarters, Sean said, "This case is tough."

Sheena murmured, "We were not called in for nothing. So it is a tough nut to crack but I think we can do it."

Sean murmured, "The power of positive thinking. Yeah, I think there has to be something we overlooked. I want to talk to the staff members again."

They both entered the kitchen finding Parvati stirring a big pot of dal curry and Mala Shetty rolling out rotis deftly.

The two women greeted them politely, but their eyes were wary.

Sean perched on a kitchen stool while Sheena sat on the nearest chair.

Sean asked, "How long will you stay here?"

Mala answered, "Just for a few days. Then we will leave. I got a new job, thank god! It is in Thane and I will work as a chef for a small restaurant." She looked happy.

Sean's eyes flew to Parvati.

She shrugged, "Nothing as yet but I have hope something will turn up." But her eyes looked bleak.

Sheena asked, "Where is Gopal?"

Parvati replied, "He has gone to the village. He will be back in an hour."

"Where are the other staff?"

Mala answered, "The others are in town looking for new employment. Mohan encouraged them to go. They were worried and depressed."

Sean said, "I guess the Swami will be missed."

Parvati nodded but Mala said, "Yes, he will. But I hope you find who killed him. He did not deserve this. He was a good man. Why was he murdered? You must find the killer. I pray for him every night. He was good to us."

Sean asked, "You have absolutely no idea who could have wanted to murder him?"

Mala shook her head, "No, or else I would have told you."

Parvati, having finished cooking the dal was asked by Mala to clean the front door of the kitchen which was dirty.

Parvati obliged, going into the adjoining bathroom and fetching a scrubber and a pail of water.

She moved towards the front kitchen door and began to scrub the door, very vigorously.

Sean noticed she seemed to be a healthy and strong woman. Mala tended to be on the plump side and seemed like the type who would not be highly energetic.

They sat there for a few more minutes watching the two women, while Mala regaled them with stories about the Swami's kindness.

She told them how he had helped her son by paying his school fees for two years when her husband had died. He had told her to consider the ashram as her home. She seemed to consider him as a kind of saint and her eyes misted in remembrance.

Parvati had almost completed scrubbing the door.

The floor was wet and Sean noticed another entrance at the back, "Where does that lead to? The backyard?"

Mala nodded her head, "Yes, the backyard. The Swami used to have some chickens in the past but he had stopped keeping them for he had begun to shun meat and was turning into a vegetarian."

"We had better use that entrance since it is wet here." Sheena suggested.

Sean agreed.

Mala moved forward and opened the back door.

Outside the strong sun hit their faces. There was no breeze and the day was hot and humid.

It was a small backyard and now there were clothes lines with several wet garments hanging to dry.

Sean and Sheena glanced at them and noticed there were several shirts, sari blouses and underwear too. They then, began moving away.

Hardly had they walked a yard when Sean suddenly halted.

Sheena halted too, staring at him. Sean just stood there transfixed.

He had a strange look on his face.

He turned to Sheena after a long moment of introspection, a frown on his face. He asked, "Did you see what I saw?"

Sheena rolled her eyes, "Well, come to the point. What are you talking about?"

Sean urged her, "Think, think carefully. Cast your mind back to the courtyard. Visualise what you saw."

Sheena frowned and looked at him clueless. She said slowly, "I saw trees and lines with wet clothes." She made a move to turn around and view the backyard.

But Sean stopped her, "Not yet. This is brain storming time. Well? Think now."

Sheena thought carefully. Her mind examined the courtyard minutely. She had a very good memory and in her mind's eye she could see the backyard clearly without turning around. She remembered the wet clothes on the lines, flying very gently with the breeze.

A few minutes later her face cleared, "The underwear!"

Sean said, "Precisely, my dear! Let's take another closer look, shall we?"

The front door had been washed and both the women were in the kitchen cooking, for they could hear their voices.

Sean put his finger on his lips and Sheena understood that they ought to be quiet.

Both walked to the clothes lines. The garments were almost dry for the sun dried them up very fast.

The last line held five pairs of underwear. They were all men's underwear.

Sean examined all five quite minutely. Sheena pointed out to the last underwear on the line.

It was of average size and grey with the brand name *Mufti* on it. The others were from popular brands.

Sean quickly took it off the line and pocketed it.

So far, no one had seen them.

Then he gestured Sheena to follow him.

They both went into the ashram.

The bedroom of the Swami was locked as usual.

But Sean and Sheena entered the bedroom with the key that they possessed given to them by Inspector Kumar.

Ch 16

They shut the door and looked around. The room looked the same, quite bare, neat and clean.

Sean went into the small bathroom and found the towel hanging on the rack in its usual place. He pulled off the towel and found the grey underwear they had seen before.

Sheena stood beside him. He fished out the grey underwear from his pocket and compared the size of both. It was a perfect match!

Sean whistled under his breath. Sheena gave him a thumbs up!

"Now let's compare these with the Swami's underwear." Sheena suggested. The white underwear of the Swami's and the grey underwear were average size but the grey underwear was an inch smaller than the white underwear. This could be because the brands were different.

"Let's meet the ladies in the kitchen." Sean suggested, pocketing both the grey underwear.

Locking the bedroom, Sean and Sheena went towards the kitchen.

Parvati and Mala were engrossed with the meal preparation.

They both looked a bit hot and sweaty for the kitchen had only one small fan twirling around, which seemed to be insufficient in the heat.

Both the women looked surprised seeing them again.

Mala asked, "Is something the matter?"

Sean looked at her with a neutral expression. He said quietly, "Who hangs the clothes on the clothes lines?"

Mala looked at Parvati, "She does."

Parvati stopped chopping the tomatoes and looked at him inquiringly.

Sean produced the grey underwear from his pocket.

Parvati's mouth gaped open slightly. He dangled them in front of her, "Recognise these?"

A look of fear crept into her eyes. She said, "What…"
Mala took over in her usual bossy way, "That's Gopal's!"

Parvati darted a fearful look at her and she seemed afraid.

Sean asked, "Are these your son's underwear?" Parvati nodded.

"Tell us what was your son's underwear doing in the bathroom of the Swami?"

Parvati shook her head wordlessly.

Sean said grimly, "This is serious. You will have to come with Gopal to the police station."

Suddenly Parvati's face crumpled, "Gopal is innocent. He has done nothing."

Sean said grimly, "Summon him and you both will come with us for questioning."

Parvati hesitated but agreed. She used her mobile and called Gopal.

He promised to come right away. When he arrived he seemed nervous but was very quiet, refusing to speak much.

Twenty minutes later, all four of them set off in the car with Alok driving to the Thane police station.

Ch 17

 Gopal and Parvati sat together in the interrogation room on the hard backed chairs. They both seemed tense but that was unsurprising given the fact that few folk ever seemed at ease in this room.

It was a silent sombre room that had a two way mirror.

Inspector Kumar stood there, sipping a cup of hot tea, watching.

Minutes later, the door opened and both the officers strode in. They sat opposite the mother and son.

Parvati said anxiously, "Sir, what is this about? We have done nothing wrong."

Sean said, "You will speak when questioned."

His tone was firm.

Parvati lapsed into silence.

Sean asked, "You agree that both these underwear are yours?" He placed both the underwear from the evidence plastic bag that he had obtained in front of Gopal.

Gopal swallowed hard, "Yes, sir. But…"

Sean put up his hand to silence Gopal, "So it is a yes."

Gopal nodded, "Yes, sir."

He looked frightened.

Sean said, "What was your underwear doing in the Swami's bathroom?" Gopal directed a quick look at Parvati. But Parvati was staring at her hands. She did not glance his way.

Gopal cleared his throat, "I do not know……. "

Sean said grimly, "I think you do know. You were there, weren't you in the bedroom that night?"

Gopal shook his head, "No, sir, I swear."

Sean said, "Hiding things will not help your case. Be truthful and things will be alright."

 Gopal shook his head stubbornly, "I did not kill him. I am innocent."

Sheena questioned Parvati, "Do you know about your son's visit to the Swami's bedroom?"

Parvati shook her head, "I know nothing."

With a hard look on his face, Sean stood up and Sheena did the same, "Very well. Both of you remain here. You will be questioned again." They both walked away, shutting the door behind them while a constable stood outside at watch.

Ch18

Inspector Kumar promptly gestured to the peon nearby to fetch them some tea.

Minutes later, sipping tea, they stood there watching the mother and son.

Gopal put his head on the table, covering his face.

Parvati seemed to be in a world of her own.

"Think one of them did it?" Inspector Kumar questioned.

Sean said, "Yes, my bet was it was Gopal."

Sheena nodded, "Most likely."

"Let them sweat. We will hold them here for two hours. They have water on the table and that's all they will get. It is my bet they will be ready to talk." Sean said grimly.

After a few more minutes, all three of them left.

Sean and Sheena went to lunch in the nearby restaurant.

They took their time eating a filling meal of chicken biryani with paneer patties.

Then they made their way back to the Thane police station.

Two hours later, they strode in the interrogation room again.

Both mother and son looked fatigued.

Gopal seemed less confident now, he looked more frightened than before.

Parvati seemed to be muttering to herself. Her anxiety was very apparent. Sean and Sheena sat opposite them.

The time was now three o' clock and the two were most likely hungry.

Sean noticed that the water glasses had been barely touched. Their anxiety was obvious.

Sean took his time pretending to open a file and look through it. Then finally after five minutes, he looked up, "Have you anything to tell us?"

Parvati shook her head, "We are innocent."

Gopal seemed withdrawn now. He just looked at the floor listlessly.

Sean said quietly, "The Swami hurt you, didn't he?"

Gopal's eyes flew to his. He flinched. "I do not knew what you mean…"

Sean said coldly, "I think you do. You were in that room that night. Your underwear is evidence. No judge or jury will believe that you had never visited the Swami's bedroom."

Gopal was silent. He suddenly said, "Let me go home."
Sean shook his head, "Tell us the truth first."

Parvati stared at her son and then looked away.

Gopal suddenly said, "Okay, I was in that bedroom. So what?"

Sean said grimly, "Why was your underwear in the bathroom?"

Gopal flushed. He suddenly blurted out, "If I tell you, will you let me go?"

Sean said grimly, "I cannot make false promises. Let me hear what you have to say."
Gopal said, "Yes, I was there that night. It was my underwear. The Swami…"

He swallowed hard. Suddenly his voice broke a bit. All at once he seemed like a vulnerable seventeen year old. He looked young and sad. The look on his face made Sheena's heart constrict but her face was cool and impassive.

He said brokenly, "After my father died…….I was very lost. The income dried up and mum took the job in the ashram. We were so happy. We had a steady income and room to stay though we had a small house in the village. The Swami seemed to like me."

He looked away, his face crumpling a bit, "I thought he was like a dad to me. I liked him and respected him. He took a lot of interest in me. He told me that he would take care of us. He wanted me to serve as his assistant. So he told me that since I had finished my schooling, I was educated enough to serve him and the community."

He paused.

He then continued, "I was ready to learn. He told my mother to let me attend this course. It would help me in understanding the job. I had to reside in the dormitory with the other men. I felt happy."

He bit his lip and looked away.

He suddenly could not speak. Tears filled his eyes. He brushed them away impatiently, swallowing hard.

Parvati touched his hand sympathetically.

He seemed to draw strength from his mother. She whispered, "Beta go on. Tell them everything. We have nothing to fear. God is our protector."

Gopal nodded. He said more confidently, "Well, two days passed and suddenly the Swami told me to come into his bedroom one night. He told me to steal away while the others were sleeping. He had something to show me."

Gopal looked at his feet sadly, "I said yes. He was like a God to me, a father too. I would have done anything for him."

He then looked at Sean, "He made me take off my clothes. He told me it was good for my spiritual awakening. I was hesitant at first but he grew angry so I obeyed him."

A sheen of moisture crept anew into his eyes, "I stood there naked and felt ashamed. He…he raped me. I tried to resist but he was too strong for me. He even caught my hair tightly and I knew he would use violence if I resisted. The rape went on for a few days. I did not tell mother. I knew she would get upset and she would lose her job. My job too. I was very upset but did not tell anyone. I felt they would not believe me. He insisted on my coming to his room every night. It was easy because at one or two at night, the men were fast asleep. Besides my bed was right next to the door and it was very easy to steal away. Only once Dighe seemed suspicious and asked me if I could not sleep because he saw me getting up. I told him that I had left the room because I needed a bed cover for my bed and that the cupboard was on the landing near the staircase. It has bed linen. You must have seen it. He believed me. After that I was more careful and began to put pillows on my bed and cover it with a sheet to make it appear that I was sleeping. The dormitory was dark because the curtains were thick and drawn at night and there was no night lamp on so no one noticed I was not really in my bed."

Gopal paused.

Parvati looked stricken.

Gopal darted a glance at her and seemed to draw strength from her face. He was apparently very close to her.

He took a sip of water from the glass nearby as if he wanted a break.

Sean and Sheena did not hurry him up. They knew he would tell all if they were patient and not too aggressive. Perhaps the presence of Sheena soothed him for Sheena despite her brisk exterior while dealing with criminals could also look quite warm and friendly when she chose to.

He looked at Sheena and continued, "So I met him every night. But on the night before the murder night…..he was very….." Gopal flushed. "He made me do things that were demeaning. He made me do acts that were getting more and more repulsive. I hated him. I hated him so much. The worst thing was that he wanted to film me naked and pose for his private collection. He would use his mobile and film me. I pretended to agree but asked him that since I was very tired that day, I would do this the next night. He wanted to argue but since I pretended to be very sleepy, he agreed very reluctantly."

Gopal paused. He swallowed hard, "The next day, I helped mum in the kitchen with the washing up and sweeping of the staff quarters. I was very upset. Even mother asked me what was the matter. But I just told her I was feeling tired. She was busy that day making some dosas and did not press me further. I thought about it and rage filled me. I knew I could not bear it anymore. I hated him so much, I wanted to kill him. So I made up mind that he should die. What he did to me was repulsive. We were poor, we needed the money so he took advantage of me. I planned to kill him. The underwear you found was what he wanted. He had asked me to keep one pair of underwear in his bathroom so that he could touch it and fantasise about me. It was so sick but I agreed. He was such a pervert." He paused and looked at trembling hands.

"I took a rock from the garden before I went to his room and I hid it below his window at a corner. As soon as he finished sex with me, he wanted to film me. He wanted to use the bathroom. So when he was in the bathroom, I jumped out of the window and brought the rock with me. It was heavy and I somehow managed. I kept it behind the bed, knowing he might not spot it immediately. He went to get his mobile from the side-table. I could not bear him filming me. His back was turned. I knew I had to act fast. I wanted him dead. I was too upset to think. I grabbed the rock and I bashed his head, with all my might. He groaned and he staggered. I bashed it again and he fell to the floor. I knew he was dead because of the blood and the glazed sightless look in his eyes. I did not wait. I did not remember he had my underwear because I had no idea he had kept the underwear behind the towel rack. I escaped and ran up to my room. I jumped on the bed and lay there. I could not sleep that night."

Gopal gave a sob, "I confessed. You may ask me if I regret this. No, he deserved it. He abused me, he demeaned me. I cannot forgive him."

He began now to sob loudly, burying his face in his hands. He looked vulnerable and helpless.

Sean cleared his throat and said, "You will wait here. You will stay in our custody."

Parvati was asked to go home. A defence lawyer arranged for Gopal, was a man named Basra.

Ch 19

The newspapers were filled with the news about the arrest of Gopal. However, since he was a minor then he would be tried as a minor.

Sean and Sheena returned back to Delhi within a few days.

The trial that was conducted a month later was one in which the judge seemed sympathetic with the victim.

He was to be sent to a remand home for a year but because the judge took into account his widowed mother, he told him that he would do community service for a year.

Community sentencing is a kind of punishment that includes non-custodial punishment like house arrest, curfew, fines etc. for those who have committed less dangerous crimes.

Gopal would be assigned an offender manager who worked for the Community Rehabilitation Company. He would not be paid for his work but his social service was a kind of compensation for his act of murder. He would be trained in a specific field during this time and thus be able to get productive employment later on.

However, Gopal's version of the story was not believed by all. Some thought that the Swami had been a good man and Gopal had fabricated the story, probably because he was a thief who thought there was cash in the Swami's room.

But many others were too ready to believe that Swami Laxman had been a paedophile and his good name was completely spoilt.

Director Verma was pleased with their success when they returned back.

He told them, "You two are a dynamic duo. Keep up the good work!"

If Sheena had seemed quiet and not her usual self, he either did not notice or refrained from commenting.

Only Sean noticed Sheena's downcast face but he did not mention it. He knew she was going through tough times. He knew she liked her career but also wanted a personal life.

The problem was- could there be a suitable compromise?

Epilogue

A month later.

Sean was sent to Hyderabad to assist the local police on a drug busting operation.

Sheena was requested not to accompany him for Director Verma wanted her to tackle the case of a child prostitute in Delhi, who had to be rescued from a brothel. He had full faith that Sheena could tackle the case.

Sheena agreed and she worked hard to rescue the child who was reported to be working in the brothel. It was a difficult case for when the police in the past had tried to find the child, the brothel pimps had cleverly hidden her from sight. The girl was just eleven years old and had been kidnapped from her village.

Sheena worked undercover posing as a journalist, trying to interview the prostitutes.

She succeeded in rescuing the child who had been hidden in a small outhouse with three other teenage girls.

All four were rescued and sent back to their parents.

Solving the case took tremendous efforts and Sheena had been successful. She had saved three other young girls besides the child and to her it was a victory.

Sean returned back two weeks later. The drug busting operation had been successful. The men involved were behind bars awaiting their trial.

Both met each other at work. Director Verma seemed happy with their success.

He said, "The two of you are a good team but at times, I will want you to work separately too."
His voice brooked no argument.

Both agreed.

After a long day, Sean asked Sheena if he could drop her home for her car had been in the garage for some minor repairs. She had come to work by cab.

She hesitated but agreed.

Sean drove along the busy streets, making casual conversation.

If he noticed that she seemed a bit withdrawn and quiet, he made no mention of this.

At her residence, he halted the car.

He looked at her as she fumbled to open her seat belt.

"How about inviting me over?" His voice was casual.

His request surprised her.

She stared at him but his gaze was impassive, revealing none of his thoughts or feelings.

She shrugged, "Well, alright."

Both of them headed to her apartment on the fifth floor of a tall high rise building. It was a well maintained building and he knew that it had belonged to her husband. Her husband had his own flat and he had given her this apartment after their divorce. He had not been a mean man in a financial way. Sean thought that she was lucky in that respect.

Her apartment was a two bedroom one, rather small but it was well decorated.

The marble flooring gave a rather posh air. The furniture did not look expensive but it suited the place perfectly. On a sideboard there were various curios and artefacts displayed.

Seeing his gaze on them, she smiled wryly, "Collected them on some of my work trips. Got so many that these days I do not buy curios anymore."

"Nice collection."

"Yes, I guess so."

She sat down on a sofa, her face looking a bit tense. She had on a light makeup and her hair was in a neat ponytail that she often wore.

He acted cool for he sensed her discomfiture.

He admired the curios for a few moments longer then sat opposite her on the red suede sofa.

 The paintings on the wall interested him for he commented, "You like art?"

Sheena nodded with a smile, "My nephew, my sister's son likes art. He paints a lot. He is just sixteen but a budding artist. I framed six of his paintings. I liked them a lot. I try to encourage him by sending paint colours on his birthday or a blank canvas too."

"Great." Sean said, stretching his long legs, looking quite at home.

Sheena felt a bit ill at ease for it felt strange having a man in her home. She had lived alone since her divorce and rarely dated. She had not entertained a man in her home but always met them outside. It felt strange that her work partner was sitting here so comfortably as if he belonged here. The thought startled her for it really seemed as if he belonged here.

She looked away thinking these days she was becoming too fanciful.

She said, "Will you have something to drink?"

Sean looked at her as she got to her feet. He knew she was uncomfortable with his presence here but was making an effort to be cordial.

He thought he knew why. Sheena did not dare hope for a romance because of their jobs. She knew it would be detrimental. The attraction between them still simmered and he knew she felt it too. That was what made it so dangerous. It was like playing with fire.

He said quietly, "Anything cool would do."

She nodded mutely and went into the small kitchen done in cream and red. It was neat and functional from what he could see since he was sitting directly opposite it.

She came back with two glasses of iced lemonade.

It looked delicious. He took it and sipping it murmured, "Tastes good."

Sheena smiled and sat down in her original place, the lemonade in her hand. She sipped it slowly, savouring its icy freshness.

She said conversationally, "You did a good job on that drug bust. Really good."

"Well, you did a good job rescuing those young kids." Sean said, raising his glass in a toast.

Sheena raised her glass.

"Here's to more success." Sean toasted with a grin.

At this words, Sheena did not smile, she merely looked at her glass reflectively.

Sensing her mood, Sean said, "Let's not talk shop."

Sheena offered a wan smile.

Sean began making casual conversation about a latest Bollywood movie he had seen on Netflix.

Since Sheena had watched it also, both spent a while discussing the movie and agreeing it had been a good movie.

An hour later, Sean said seriously, "Look, both of us agree we make a good team. We have enjoyed success. But I came here for a reason."

Sheena looked at him, feeling confused.

The cuckoo clock in the living room chimed the hour- eight o'clock.

Sean leant forward, his hands entwined loosely in front of him. He looked very serious.

He chose his words carefully, "Sheena, you must know that it is hard working with you day after day in close proximity."

Sheena's eyes widened. She just looked at him. The vulnerability on her face touched a chord in his heart.

He went on, his eyes on her, "The reason being is that I am attracted to you. I know we have this mutual attraction."

He suddenly looked at his hands, "But…" He flushed a bit.

Sheena had never seen him looking so discomfited before. He seemed totally ill at ease.

Sheena did not say anything, knowing it was prudent for him to speak his mind.

Sean finally looked straight at her, their eyes meeting. He seemed awkward as if what he was trying to tell her was very difficult for him. This captured her attention more than if he had been more vocal.

He chose his words carefully, "Okay, what I am trying to say is…."

Suddenly, he made a sound of frustration.

He raked his fingers through his hair and seemed to come to a decision.

He got to his feet and joined her on the long sofa. He faced her and their eyes met.

Her eyes were wide with anxiety and he seemed then to relax.

He took her hands in his and felt their softness tremble.

He said softly, "I care for you, Sheena. I care a hell lot for you."

At her surprised expression, he went on, "I will be truthful. I love you." After he had uttered these words, he relaxed visibly as if the hardest part was done with.

Suddenly a glimmer of a smile touched her lips, and he drew courage from it.

"Sheena, if you want I could go down on my bloody knees and propose but I am not such a romantic kind of guy. I want to marry you. Sheena, will you marry me? For god's sake, say yes."

Sheena looked at their entwined hands and then raised her dark, expressive kohl rimmed eyes, "Will we be able to work together?"

Sean said grimly, "Most likely. I know you want kids, you desire a family life. If I am wrong then I promise, I will leave and never talk about this again."

The silence in the room was deafening. Sheena did not look at him.

Sean sat still, looking at her. She looked sad.

Sheena said, "You are right. I desire kids, a family life. I thought my career was everything but there are so many sacrifices, I do not think it is that worth it anymore."

She smiled wryly, "Maybe I am becoming old. But yes, I think the answer is yes."

Their eyes met.

Sean said, "You have not said whether you care for me. But that does not matter because I know we like each other. That's a start."

Sheena suddenly gave him a playful hit on his arm, "My, my, the great Sean Fernandez acting so humble! "

Sean flushed.

Sheena leant close to him and said huskily, "Don't you know that I care for you? I care a lot. Do you think I would give up my career for nothing?"

Sean bent down and brushed his lips against hers. "We could still work together till you want to give up. I know Director Verma would permit it. What he objects to is romance not marriage."

"Yes, I think so too."

When he kissed her again, she knew with certainty that he truly cared for her.

Sean said, "I have a small flat and I do not think you will be happy there. So I am going to buy a new home for us. A friend of mine, an old school chum is migrating to Australia. He has a small cottage just two miles from here. It is in a quiet area. A nice garden, not too big but big enough. I can afford the price he is offering. I told him to keep it on hold for me and I could tell him tomorrow morning."

Sheena said mischievously, "So if I refused, then you would not buy it?"

Sean kissed her hard, "That's for teasing me. But yeah, I would change my mind. I gave all this very good thought."

"You never do things in half measure." Sheena commented.

"You got that right. So is it a yes? I mean I would like to show it to you."

Sheena touched his hand, "I will rely on your good judgement. It should be a surprise."

Sean nodded a bit uncertainly, "It is fully furnished. I saw it and like it. "

Sheena laughed, "Don't worry, I will like it too."
Sean kissed her again, "Your lips are so kissable!'

They spent the next three minutes kissing. Sean then looked at her upturned face and her moist expressive eyes, "I love you. After marriage would you still like to work with me?'

Sheena thought it over, "Yes, but you know what? We will work together for a few years then I will take a long break, have those kids I always wanted. If I ever miss my career, I will return. If Director Verma objects, we will work separately but I will not give up my job so soon. Fair?"
Sean hugged her, "I never want you to get depressed about any decision.

Your happiness is mine."

Sheena nestled in his arms contentedly, "Sean Fernandez, did anyone tell you that you worry too much? Just trust me, let's go with the flow of life. I have this feeling we will be very happy. Hmmm…. Mrs Sheena Fernandez….. I intend to take your surname. It sounds just right, doesn't it?"

"Just perfect!"

And their lips clung tenderly together again.

Outside through the open window, there appeared a cluster of visible stars twinkling happily in the sky, radiating soft light that had permeated the shadowy night sky.

Sheena nestled in Sean's arms and knew come what may, she had found a partner for life.

The End.